Living With Grace

Living With Grace

Memories of Food, Family, Friendship and Faith

Sheryl Rooth

Dedication

To my husband John, who supports every crazy idea that I have, like this one, without hesitation or condition.

To my daughter Samantha Grace, who inherited her Great-Gram's patience for baking from scratch, her musical talent and the courage to follow her own path.

To my son Haydn Sidney, who inherited his Great-Gram's creative soul, her quick laugh and flair for drama.

To my Gram, who I miss every single day. Thank you for all of it.

I love you.

Table of Contents

The F Word

Simpler days. How many of us long for those, now? In a time where it's a twisted badge of honour to brag about how busy you are, secretly many of us long for those less committed and less technology-driven days as years gone by. You prioritized your time differently, maybe a little more carefully or thoughtfully.

As a kid, I spent a considerable amount of my life on my grandparents' farm in Newark, Ontario. There was no such thing as the internet. No cell phones. Heck, sometimes my grandparents didn't even have cable! Farm life revolved around chores, church and really good food. You made your own fun and along the way, you learned some life lessons that were not necessarily by accident but sometimes they were. My grandmother, Grace, taught me more about family, faith, friendship, and food than any textbook ever did. She was the teacher she always wanted to be, she just didn't have a typical classroom.

My grandmother's lessons were clear. Your family comes first. Your faith will bring the friendships both with God and with others. The food will bring them all together, no matter what their beliefs. Like a good pecan pie, the more nuts you can crowd together in one place, the crunchier it will be. (this analogy should not be used if you are allergic to nuts).

Even after her death, Gram is still teaching me lessons. For example how you can mix almost anything with Jell-O and call it a salad. That she believed in equal rights for women long before we started demanding it. That First Nations people are the true Canadians. Spirituality brings you a level of comfort to which nothing else can quite compare. Taking time to read and write out your thoughts can be therapeutic. And a successful life isn't measured by how much credit you have at the bank, but by how much you have accumulated with interest in your memory bank.

Living With Grace is a collection of memories I have of Gram on the farm, her work and her unwritten philosophies about living a long and enriched life.

When my grandparents were in their mid-80's I gave them a list of questions to answer. I needed to know more about who they were so that my children would have this family history to build upon. I didn't know then that their words would come back to be shared in this way but I do enjoy the serendipitous results that give life to this story. A life that wasn't always perfect. It certainly wasn't always happy, but when it came to our time together, she never let that show. These are the heartfelt stories, devotionals and of course, the recipes that she cherished the most, folded together with a little humour to keep it sweet.

Chapter One

Slip and Slide

When my grandmother, Grace Roberts (hereafter referred to as Gram) passed away at the age of 98, my family was tasked with cleaning out her belongings from the Tillsonburg, Ontario home she shared with my grandfather Sidney Roberts (hereafter referred to as Poppa Sid), who had passed away two years prior. After 74 years of marriage, they had accumulated many treasures. As people often do, over the years they had downsized their possessions as they moved. That didn't make cleaning out their home any less arduous, but it was a much appreciated slip and slide down memory lane. There were so many items that held memories large and small, for decades of my life. My grandparents meant the world to me, my grandmother in particular was a constant throughout my life. I didn't realize just how many lessons I'd learned until she was gone. Isn't that always the way with life and death? We take for granted the moments we have and we later regret the ones we let slip through our fingers.

For months, Gram had painstakingly gone through the house and placed yellow sticky notes on almost everything. In her unmistakable handwriting, the notes held the names of her children and grandchildren. Everywhere you looked there was a note. On the paintings and the china cabinets. Even the salt and pepper shakers. Every room looked like a confetti canon had been discharged. It was a good thing she didn't have a cat, for it too would have been designated with a note on its tail. Right to the end this woman was organized.

A few years earlier, she and Poppa Sid had asked us all what we would like to have from their home after they passed. I think they wanted to avoid any uncomfortable family disagreements. I also think they were a little tickled to know that there were certain items that held sentimental value to us or historical family value that we knew nothing about.

How do you answer a question like that and not sound ungrateful or greedy? Coming to terms with the fact that the two most influential people in my life were going to leave me quite soon, was difficult enough. Trying to be fair to my siblings on top of that realization seemed impossible.

Eventually, this persistent duo got the answers they were looking for, hence the carefully placed sticky notes. If you were really fortunate, your designated items also had a second note with them, explaining the history of how it came in to their hands. Family heirlooms from names a hundred years old. Milestone anniversary gifts, paintings, clocks, china, all items that were woven into the daily fabric of their marriage of 74 years.

Packing up those belongings was a front row seat on an emotional roller coaster for me. So many happy memories connected with even the most mundane item. Like a hand-held eggbeater that brought howls of laughter from my sister and I as we remembered spending what seemed like days beating egg whites until they were stiff enough for Gram's lemon meringue pie. Looking back, those egg whites were plenty stiff. It was a ruse to keep little girls busy for awhile longer.

As we went from room to room, filling box after box, I came across so many different aspects of Gram's life. Items that represented the things she did that made her whole. She was a wife, a mother, a grandmother and a great-grandmother but she was so much more than these important roles.

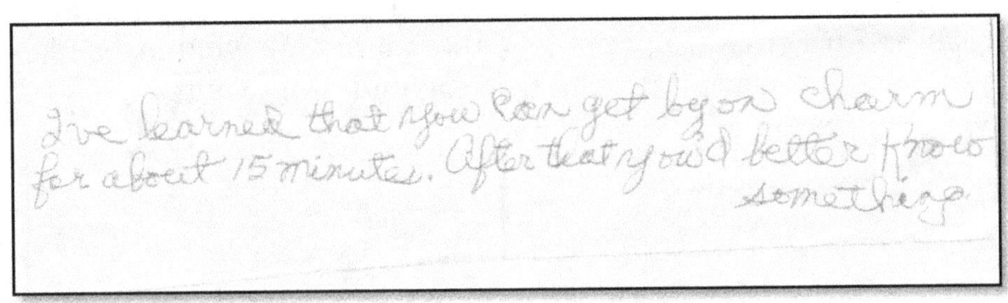

For a good chunk of my childhood, my grandparents lived on a farm in Newark, Ontario. This is the place I spent the most time with my Gram and the memories that make me smile whenever I pass a golden hay field. It was there in the country that it seemed to me she was the happiest. Where in my eyes, she made the best out of everything.

In the country is where she reinforced her faith and her place with God. Farm life was where she seemed to discover her life's purpose. Every day brought new adventures, challenges and opportunities to grow more than crops and children. She grew as a person.

In a closet, I found boxes and large manila envelopes of her writings. Poetry, news articles, skits and recitations she had given from a very young age up into her eighties. All handwritten. I found her diaries, with decades of history and observation behind the brass clasps. The tin box that held the secret family recipes. My great grandmother's well-stained and well-used recipe book as well as scrapbooks and photo albums full of black and white memories of days gone by.

On the table beside her rocking chair with the worn, wooden arms was a bowl full of strips of paper. I picked out a few and held them in my hands, slowly opening each one. Every strip contained a hand-written quote, a quip or verse that she took comfort in or made her chuckle. Her daily affirmations I suppose. I collected them all, some so old the paper was yellowing and the lettering faded, and placed them in an envelope to pore through later.

As we finished packing up each room, each of us taking what was left to us and what was cherished most, it felt strange. Ninety-eight years of life now contained in Xerox paper boxes and set to travel down the 401 and to the Tillsonburg Salvation Army Thrift Store. Our car and trailer were packed so full that my husband insisted we would have to leave our children behind if I wanted to bring

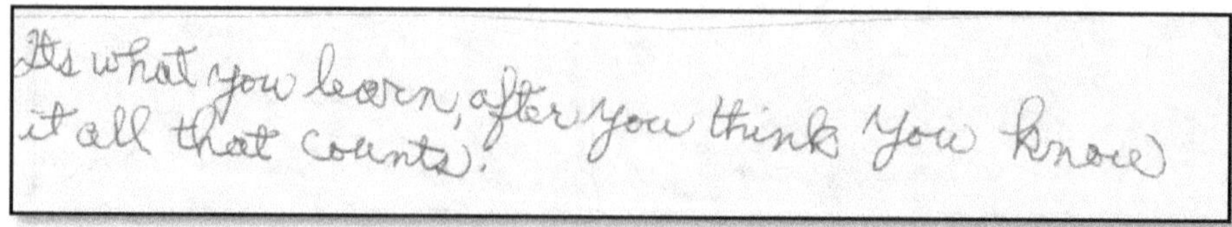

anything else home. He was right; of course, I couldn't keep it all and besides, I liked our kids. I was however, hesitant to leave anything. I was afraid that if I never saw that item again, I might lose the precious memory that was connected to it.

Some memories do fade quickly, like the sound of someone's laugh or the way they said "hello" when they answered the telephone. They're not always attached to a tangible item you can hold in your hand. I'm slowly parting with some of the furnishings and odds and ends that I felt I just had to have in that moment of grief and nostalgia.

It's taken me years to sort through all of these gifts Gram left behind. From the little notebook from the 1930's with stories written in pencil, to the sermons she gave as a guest speaker at her church, with each one, I revised the story of the woman that I thought I knew. An even more interesting and multi-dimensional woman who was maybe a little more ahead of her time than I gave her credit for. She was a feminist long before there was a word for it. She believed in raising women up to be equal with men, while still taking comfort in the traditional expectations that brought her happiness.

What lies ahead in these pages are the things which lifted her up. It is what helped to make her the woman she was. These are what built the foundation of my childhood on the farm and the memories of a grandmother I was so fortunate to have.

Grace and her grandchildren, 1973

Chapter Two

In the Beginning
(That's original)

Bella Grace was born on December 1, 1914 and was the second of four children in the Millard family. It was a terribly kept family secret that she hated the name Bella and only responded to Grace. She would never believe me anytime I told her how common that name had become, by 2009 it had a 167% increase in popularity, but she was having have none of it. She was and always would be Grace.

She grew up in the Foldens community with her siblings Carl, George and June and her parents George Earl and Vera. According to Gram her father was a second-generation farmer and her mother was "a wonderful cook,

Grace (left) and June, early 1940's

14

a great seamstress, a good housekeeper, a community and church worker who expected the best of her family and was often disappointed." Some things never change.

Hill On Way To Port Burwell A Challenge For Tin Lizzie
Grace Roberts - The London Free Press - Saturday June 5, 1999

Our family and several neighbour families got to go on a very special picnic once every summer during the 1920's. This special place was Port Burwell on Lake Erie.

On a July Sunday morning, my father got the Model T Ford gassed up and made sure the tires were roadworthy while my mother packed a big lunch.

Three "Tin Lizzies" in a row set off at 9am. We lived 65 kilometres from the lake and we had to be there before noon.

All went well until we got to Tillsonburg. As we headed south from there, the narrow road and surroundings were like a desert. The trail snaked along the edges of deep gulleys causing us to fear going over the edges. We finally reached Straffordville; the hills got higher, the gulleys deeper.

One hill in particular was so high the Model T refused to go up. We all got out of the car except father and walked to the top while he drove up. Eventually, close to noon, we arrived at the park overlooking the lake. Picnic tables were soon covered with cloths and lots and lots of food and we were all so hungry.

Our parents made us wait an hour before going in the water.

We had a glorious time, splashing, jumping the waves and making sand castles. At 4:30pm we had to leave the lake behind and head for home, hopefully arriving before dark.

My memory of the return trip is a blur. I fell asleep shortly after

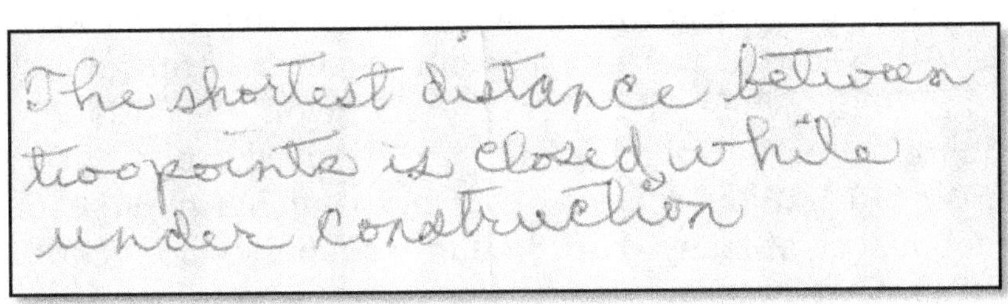

Sid, Grace and brother George (right), 1940's

leaving, dreaming of the next summer when we would do it all over again.

The 1920's were revolutionary times for women in Canada. Member of Parliament Agnes MacPhail, the first woman to be elected to the House of Commons got the pay equity ball rolling (and it only took three decades to become legislation!).

Women were soon to be declared "persons" under the law thanks to the Alberta "Famous Five" women activists (Emily Murphy, Henrietta Muir Edwards, Nellie McClung, Louise Crummy McKinney and Irene Parlby) who fought for decades for equality. I can't imagine being a young woman like my Gram, discovering a new-found freedom to be whatever you dreamed of being and not what was expected of you. It would have been exhilarating and daunting at the same time, your family expecting you to be one woman because that's what society has dictated for centuries but in your heart and your mind, you have different aspirations. Perhaps it's why she was so excited when I was accepted into university and so deeply disappointed when I flunked out.

Gram learned at the apron strings of her mother. At the age of 14 in 1928, Gram started working as a housekeeper earning $4.00 per week. In 1935, when she was 21, she won the title of Miss Tillsonburg at the Tillsonburg Fair. She received a prize of $10.00 and a sash. Much to the chagrin of her husband, her photo ended up in the footlocker of many Oxford County soldiers who went to war just a few short years later. A feminist today looking at these choices Gram made almost a hundred years ago - the job, the contest - might not see these as power moves, but I see it differently. She made the choice to do all of these things. They were the beginning of what was yet to come.

Artwork by a young Grace, 1927

Sheryl Rooth

Dad's Got the Rheumatiz
Grace Millard - Early 1930's

The baby's got the hoopin' cough

And Sammy's got the flu

Most everything at our house

Has lately gone askew

Sylvester's got the measles now

and so has Sister Liz

But these are merely trifles

Dad has got the rheumatiz

The baby with the hoopin' cough is hoopin' night and day

Ol' Doctor Brown is tryin' hard to drive the cough away

There's lots of trouble brewin' but the worstest thing what is

My dad is in such awful pain, he's got the rheumatiz

There's Sammy with the pesky flu

Had ought to be in bed, Ma says

But he prefers to mope around the house instead.

But after all flu ain't so bad, there's troubles worse than this

Enough to drive one crazy - Dad has got the rheumatiz

My Ma hain't got the hoopin' cough nor measles nor her flu

Nor I ain't either but we both are feelin' purty blue

I'm subject to the measles though but what of that, gee whiz!

I'll stand most anything but say, I don't want the rheumatiz.

The Tramp
Grace Millard - 1931 Junior Farmer's League

Lemme sit down a minute,
A stone's got into my shoe.
Don't you commence your cussin'
I ain't done nothin' to you.

I'm a tramp, what of it?
Folks say we're no good.
But tramps have to live I reckon,
Though folks don't think we should.

Down in the Le-High Valley,
Where me and my people grew
I was a blacksmith captain,
Yes, and a good one too.

There was me and my wife and Nellie.
Nellie was just sixteen.
And she was the prettiest critter,
The Valley had ever seen.

Boys, why she had a dozen.
And them from near and far.
But they were mostly farmers
And none of them suited her.
There was a city stranger,
brave, handsome and tall.
Blame him. I wish I had him
strangled against that wall.

He was the man for Nellie.
Nellie, she knew no ill.
Mother, she tried to stop it
But you know young gals, will.

He was a soft-tongued villain
And got her to run away.
More than a month thereafter
We heard from the poor young thing.
He had ran away and left her
Without a wedding ring.

Back to her home we brought her.
Back to her mother's side.
Filled with a raging fever,
She fell at my feet and died.
Frantic with shame and trouble
Her mother begins to sink.
Dead, in less than a fortnight
That's when I took to drink.
Give me one glass, Colonel,
And I'll be on my way.
And I'll tramp 'til I find the scoundrel
If it takes to the Judgement Day.

I've learned that education, experience, and memories are 3 things no one can take away from you.

Chapter Three

When Boy Meets Girl

While she was living in the town of Ingersoll Ontario, Gram met my Poppa Sid. At the time, in 1934 or so, Ingersoll had a population of around 5,200 and provided many wholesome activities and events for young people to mix and mingle.

Sid and Grace met at the Fireman's Ball in the Old Town Hall and the rest, as they say, is history.

Poppa Sid reminisced "Well, I saw Grace at this dance and she was alone, so I asked her to dance. I thought that she was beautiful, very good looking, a little shy at first. We got going on walks and talks. Of course, she'd love a kiss or two."

When I asked my Gram why she chose my grandpa, she said "I fell in love with Sid, first he was so good looking, wavy hair, tall and straight, dressed so smart. I just knew he was honest by his eyes. He was good natured, a great sense of humour, not braggy and boy could he kiss!"

So as I see it, there are three key components to a happy marriage: must love to dance, be good looking and have exceptional kissing ability. Of course, you need much more to build a foundation for a marriage of 74 years than a burst of oxytocin, but it's a very good start.

They were married at the preacher's home in Delhi, Ontario at 6pm on Tuesday November 3, 1936. The brides' mother served "a great roast chicken dinner with all the trimmings." It was their favourite meal throughout their marriage.

My grandfather said that Gram "deserved a gold medal for what we had to do with when we got married." I think she was more than ready for that marathon with the man that she loved.

Sid and Grace, 1930's.

Can You Remember When Life Was Simple?
Grace Roberts

Memory is the mansion of the spirit. The longer you live the more rooms that mansion has, rooms with views from yesterday's windows, rooms with hearths where the heart can still warm itself with the glow from bygone fires.

You've built yourself quite a house of the mind if you can look back and remember.

When you were a business success if you had a roll top desk and a wooden waste paper basket.

When clerks wore celluloid collars from which dirt could be removed with a pencil eraser so they wouldn't have to put on a clean shirt every day.

When only really wealthy people complained about income taxes.

When even the healthiest child's nose seemed to run all winter long and for every kid who took vitamin pills there were a hundred more who still took good old undiluted cod liver oil and a dose of salt once a week as the norm.

When it was possible to go through life without ever filling out a government form and one of the arguments for having a large family was that you would always plan on living with one of your children when you grow old and not have to enter the poor house.

When many farmers thought it immoral and a sin against nature to turn good pasture land into a golf course, since nobody would use it but the idle rich.

When many a farm boy learned about women by studying the underwear ads in the mail order catalogue.

When friends could always tell when you'd been to the barbershop, because you came back smelling different.

When a wise father always gave his small son a dime to put in the church collection plate on Sunday because he knew if he gave the lad two nickels, God might wind up with only one.

When the neighbourhood iceman's horse wore a straw hat to protect him from the summer heat.

And do you remember when life was so simple that even your telephone number had only three digits.

*If a fellow expected to cut much of a swath in college with the ladies, he had to learn to play the ukulele. **

When nobody who performed a service for you would think of taking your money without saying "thank you" and meaning it?

Those were the good old days, remember?

**With excerpts from September 27, 1966 - The Indiana Gazette, Indiana, Pennsylvania*

Chapter Four

Happy House, Happy Spouse

Who knew that one Fireman's Ball could lead to over seven decades of wedded bliss?

Of course, anyone who has ever been married for more than five minutes understands that wedded bliss is a misnomer. No one stays blissful every single day of their lives. Somehow though, Sid and Grace made it work better than most.

They started their lives together in Ingersoll and bought their first home there. My Gram recalled, "It cost $1200.00. It was a 50 year old, 1½ storey frame house. Structurally, it was really sound but there was no plumbing, no heating system, one cold water tap in the kitchen, and the basement hadn't been dugout except for one small area with a dirt floor. It had lovely, wide, stained dark woodwork, 8½ foot ceilings, three bedrooms and one closet." Leave it to Gram to find the positives in what was essentially a log cabin that may or may not have had decent trim and one water source. It must have been love.

They lived frugally, they worked hard and created a happy life for themselves. They saved up their money and bought their first car in 1942. It was "a 1932 Chev Coupe with a rumble seat and six wire wheels that we purchased for $275.00". They went to the movies when they had the money and went dancing whenever they possibly could. The sweetest music this side of heaven, by the one and only Guy Lombardo who was the entertainer of choice.

Over the years, they moved a few times. They ran a small grocery store and started raising a family. Yet it didn't matter where they lived or how happily, country life called Gram's name.

Sheryl Rooth

The farm house. Judging by the pink flamingos, this is early 1970's.

Sid in the farm field, 1955

Living With Grace

The Country Offers Beauty and Peace
Grace Roberts - The London Free Press - October 4, 1956

Editor, Free Press - I just couldn't let Margaret Godfrey's article in Weekend go unchallenged. Probably the location one chooses when he moves to the country has a great bearing on whether or not he finds happiness there. However, I wish to repudiate by giving you my version on why "We moved To the Country and Are Still There".

I lived, not in a city but a large town for 25 years. True, I was born on a farm but left there at a tender age. My husband was born in the city and lived there his entire life until he also got the craze for a home in the country.

We owned and operated a small general store on a side street in the town where we lived and on Sunday and Wednesday afternoons we would drive through the country within a radius of 50 miles, trying to find something "for sale" that would suit us. One day, after months of searching we saw one that suited us. We made inquiries and discovered the little white bungalow was vacant and the owner would sell.

The house was on a 50-acre farm with beautiful rolling hills and a cool, green grove of maples. There was a barn, not too good, but usable. Also a very rickety garage which we jokingly say we have to keep the car in "to hold it up." The house was equipped with a bathroom, furnace and kitchen cupboards but was badly in need of decorating from basement to attic.

It was with misgivings we departed from our home of 17 years on a rainy Saturday night on June 26, two years ago, with our cocker spaniel and our two children, Carol aged 11 and Peter, 10 months. By the time we rolled into our beds that night we were almost unconscious from fatigue, excitement and anticipation. We awoke in the morning to the patter of rain drops on our roof. We looked out the windows in every direction and glowed with pride as we realized that the land for a half mile on either side and at the back of our house actually belonged to us.

Being in modest circumstances, my husband (Sid), took a job butchering and clerking in a large store about four miles from our farm. As the days grew into weeks, we found ourselves surrounded by a community of warm friendly folks, who did everything possible to make us feel at home. In rural communities life generally revolves

around the church. Our neighbours invited us to attend church and although we were not habitual church-goers, we soon found ourselves hating to miss a Sunday in the warm friendly atmosphere of this little country church. We now belong to several clubs in connection with the church and find them most interesting.

Carol, who is now 13 is ready to begin high school in September. She will go by bus. Carol took her grade seven and eight in our small country school where the teacher taught all grades from one to eight. I must say, she never got better marks nor more individual attention all the time she attended town school.

Sid has a second-hand tractor and a few second-hand implements and by hiring a little help, manages to grow a nice lot of cash crops and keep his job as well. This year we had 10 acres of wheat, just finished having it combined. I wish Margaret Godfrey could have seen it. It was, indeed, a picture from its rich verdant green in the late autumn and early spring to its deep golden harvest glow. We also have a few acres of peas for a local canning company and some oats and hay. Sid keeps some sows in the barn and every few months we have some of the cutest little newborn piglets you ever saw.

Perhaps I'm painting the picture too rosy, because of course, everything has its drawbacks. For instance, three weeks after we moved here the well that was connected up with the house went dry. There is another drilled well but it was at the barn 300 feet away. We didn't feel we could afford to have a ditch digger dig from the barn to the house so Sid went at it. It was very hot and very dry and he was not accustomed to this work. After two weeks of strenuous labour, we had the water at our kitchen sink once again. This is only one of many such experiences we encountered.

In spite of that we believe that anyone who is truly desirous of a country home will see so much of nature's handiwork they will be able to stand the drawbacks.

We have our own beautiful garden which we never had room for in town. We have a lovely lawn and nice flowers. Of course, these things represent lots of back-breaking labour, but oh, it is so gratifying.

We have decorated our house throughout all ourselves and painted the trim on the outside. I never made homemade bread before but I'm making it now and the children love it. We find ourselves doing all manners of things we thought we weren't capable of. Yes, our hydro goes off frequently and if it happens at mealtime we just set up the camp stove in the basement and the children think we are having a picnic. If it happens at night we light several candles and gather round the piano for a sing-song and find it quite refreshing and relaxing after watching TV for evenings on end.

In my opinion, rural life offers much more for our growing children than city life. There are no juvenile delinquents in this community. We have good clubs and organizations for young folks to belong to.

Educational opportunities are as close as the bus that goes by our door. There are lots of small tasks for country children They are never at loose ends like many city dwellers.

If we get a hankering to go to the city we can hop in the car and be there in half an hour. When we go to visit my sister and my two brothers in their beautiful, expensive homes in Toronto, our little white bungalow in the middle of nowhere seems like a haven of contentment when we return.

What if there are a few flies and bugs? The pure, clear air, the unobstructed view and a complete rainbow after a storm, the glow of the rising sun and the gold of the setting sun make a few flies seem very insignificant. I love the country.

Grace in the farm field, 1955

Prize Winning Bread

½ Cup Warm Water
1 Teaspoon Sugar
1 Envelope Of Quick Acting Yeast
2½ Cups Homogenized Milk
5 Tablespoons Sugar
5 Teaspoons Salt
1 Cup Boiling Water
5 Tablespoons Shortening
12 Cups All Purpose Or Bread Flour

In a small bowl, combine the ½ cup warm water and 1 teaspoon sugar. stir and sprinkle yeast on the surface of the liquid. let stand 10 minutes.
Scald milk. stir in 5 tablespoons of sugar and 5 teaspoons of salt. cool until lukewarm.
In a large bowl, dissolve shortening in the boiling water. cool to lukewarm and combine with milk. stir in two cups of flour and beat to form a smooth dough.
Stir the yeast mixture well and mix into the dough.
Beat in 4 cups of flour. beat vigorously until the mixture is very smooth and elastic.
Work in the remaining flour (6 cups) and knead until it is smooth and springy to the touch (the more kneading the better).
Place dough in a large, greased bowl. grease the top of the dough lightly. cover and let rise in a warm place, away from drafts until almost doubled in size.
Punch down and divide the dough into 4 round balls and cover lightly with waxed paper for 10 to 15 minutes.
Shape into loaves. placed into greased loaf pans and grease tops. let rise until doubled.
Bake at 400° for 35 minutes or until bread is firm, has come away from the edge of the pan and sounds hollow when lightly knocked with the knuckles.

Great Grandma Millard's Bran Muffin and Ginger Snap recipes

Chapter Five

Tea, Toast and Tall Tales

Mornings on the farm always began with the sound of the Black Forest cuckoo clock letting sleepyheads know it was time to rise and shine. Every hour on the hour that little white bird would pop out of the window of that wee polished wooden house and chirp an inexplicably loud "cuckoo cuckoo".
The weights on the chains were shaped like heavy pinecones and it was a coveted job to get to carefully pull the chains to wind the clock.

On the farm, mornings were my favourite part of the day. By the time I rolled my red head down the stairs and slid along on the hardwood floor to the table, my Poppa Sid would have finished the chores in the barn and be dressed for work at Maedels Grocery in Norwich, Ontario.

The smell of freshly percolated coffee hung in the air. The table was covered in a crisp, clean tablecloth. Jars of homemade strawberry jam and marmalade would sit next to the aluminum butter dish that looked like a 1950's flying saucer. The curtains would be wide open in the dining room with the fields on display. The budgie would be chirping cheerfully from his perch. It was the same scenario every morning and there was a comfort to that consistency.

After she saw Poppa Sid off to work, my Gram would toast herself a slice of Hollywood brand bread with the sesame seeds sprinkled on top, and brew some black tea in her little silver teapot. She would place a teacup and saucer on her placemat and mine. My grandparents used the same set of dishes for as long as I could remember. It was a set of china called Watermill Brown by Johnson Brothers and it depicted a small village with a river and a mill. As my grandparents aged, they mixed in some dishes that weren't quite so heavy, but the set always remained in the cupboard. Over the years, the set got a little smaller as pieces were broken or inadvertently given away. Gram never know how much I loved them. I was devastated to learn that she sold some at a garage sale. I didn't much care for the idea of strangers eating off of those dishes.

The set seemed so grown up and fancy. Coming from a house with three little kids, fancy was not something that was pulled out of the cupboard very often, if ever. If it wasn't brought to you by Tupperware or Corelle, it didn't last long in my house.

Gram never used the teacup without the saucer. You couldn't place your used teaspoon on the tablecloth. I mean, really, we weren't cavemen.

As the tea brewed, we would chat a little about what we were going to accomplish that day. We'd talk about how high the crops were or how loud the cicadas were humming so early in the morning. It seemed like an eternity waiting for the tea to be poured into our cups.

Sometimes we would have sugar cubes for our tea, as proper ladies do. Cream or milk was always served in the little matching creamer. The tea would steam as we sweetened our morning treat. It wasn't the tea I cared for though. In fact, there weren't enough sugar cubes in the world to appease my unrefined palate. What kept me captivated is what happened when the tea had been drained from the cup.

Gram would swirl the last bit of liquid around in her cup and carefully let the last dribbles into her saucer. What remained at the bottom of the cup was the beginning of the future. She would hand it to me, rest her hands in her lap and ask me, "Well, what does my future hold?" The tea leaves would tell all.

My goodness, what a heady responsibility! Reading the tea leaves and telling the future of the woman I looked to for all the answers was quite a big deal. What if the leaves told me something terrible was going to happen?

Let me clarify, I was never gifted any real psychic abilities. I grew up in an era where pop culture depicted Bigfoot encounters as a very real possibility and quicksand was a credible threat. So the very unlikely prospect of truly predicting the future from some soggy vegetation in a teacup never for a moment occurred to me.

My imagination ran wild and Gram encouraged the acceleration. She let me take on the role of fortune teller with an open mind and an open heart.

Gram's teapot and Watermill cup and saucer.

I don't recall any of my predictions or whether or not they ever came true. I'm certain they were long, drawn-out explanations of what would be sure to come, according to the magical messages in the tea leaves. I do however, have memories of a warm kitchen, the scent of toast and jam and Gram's laugh at my storytelling. I'll take that over a Bigfoot encounter any day.

Rhubarb Marmalade

1 Lemon, with peel sliced thin and chopped
1 Orange, with peel sliced thin and chopped
4 Cups Rhubarb chopped
5 Cups White Sugar
1 Cup Water
1 Cup Light Raisins

In a large kettle, mix lemon and orange with water and simmer for ten minutes over medium heat.

Add rhubarb and sugar and boil for 15-20 minutes.

Drop a teaspoon of mixture into a small bowl to see if it is starting to set.

Add raisins and boil for an additional 5 minutes.

Pour and seal in sterile jars.

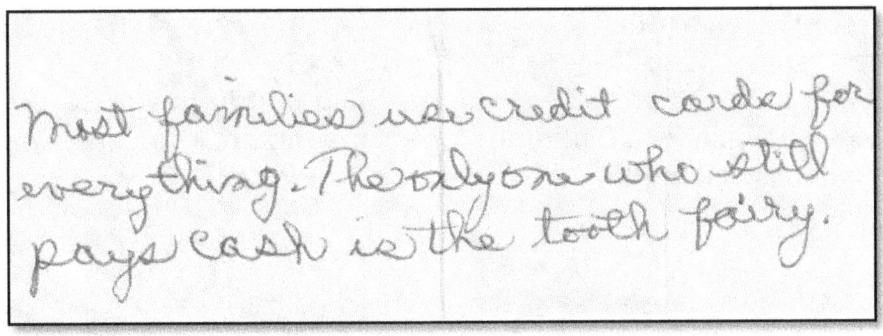

Bran Muffins

1 Cup All Bran/Bran Buds style cereal
1 Cup Boiling Water
1 Tablespoons Baking Soda
½ Cup Butter or Margarine (room temperature)
1½ Cup Granulated Sugar
2 eggs
1 Cup Raisins
2 Cups Buttermilk
2½ Cups Cake and Pastry Flour
1 Teaspoon Salt
2 Cups Bran Flakes Cereal

In a large bowl, mix together All Bran cereal, boiling water and baking soda and set aside.

In a large mixing bowl, cream together the butter and sugar. Blend in the eggs. add the All Bran mixture, raisins and buttermilk. mix well.

Beat in flour and salt into the mixture until there are no lumps. Fold in the Bran Flakes.

The batter will be thin but it will thicken as it rests. allow the batter to rest for 2 hours, refrigerated.

Preheat oven to 400°.

Spoon mixture into paper cupcake lined muffin tins to ¾ of the way full. Bake for 20 minutes for a large muffin, 18 minutes for a medium sized muffin.

Chapter Six

The Jell-O Years

I was very happy to receive the official Jell-O® bowl. Every family has official bowls. It is one bowl that has multi-purpose potential but is designated for one, possibly two clear tasks. For example, the family popcorn bowl and/or the barf bowl. Same bowl, dual purpose but always and only for those two specific functions. You don't make Jell-O in the barf bowl because that would be absurd. It is however, acceptable only for popcorn because of size and heft. Listen, I don't make the family bowl rules, I just follow them.

As I put the Jell-O bowl into my own cupboard, the clear glass felt so familiar in my adult hands. As though I had only used it yesterday and not last when I was seven or eight. The bottom of the bowl had turned opaque from years and years of metal spoons stirring the crystals. I was overcome with such a new wave of sadness, one that I was not anticipating. I really believed that in the two weeks since Gram had passed, I was either numb or had accepted this outcome. Grief is such a tricky beast. It sits in the shadows, just waiting for you to find your footing so it can jump out and knock you to the ground again.

"Gram is never going to make me orange Jell-O again." I sobbed. Which of course, was ridiculous. She hadn't made me orange Jell-O in 39 years. No one said grief was logical.

The smell of orange Jell-O to this day brings me back to the kitchen on the farm. It was a big responsibility getting to stir the boiling water from the glass measuring cup together in the bowl with the gelatin. The risk of a serious burn was ever present. I'm sure I approached it with the steely brace of a thoracic surgeon and believed perhaps, that I was the bravest kid in the world for doing such a dangerous job.

Once the crystals had melted into the hot water, I could add the cold water to the bowl, but not before inhaling deeply that refreshing orange scent. Carefully, with a long wooden spoon, I mixed the key ingredients together to create that magical, wobbly treat to be eaten a few hours later after lunch.

Sometimes we would jazz it up a little with a can of mandarin oranges or if Gram was feeling especially cheeky, we'd add maraschino cherries right from the jar! Eat your heart out, Martha Stewart!

Once the concoction had been mixed, my Gram would place the Jell-O bowl into the refrigerator. I dutifully checked it every seven minutes or so to see if it was setting properly. Sometimes I would push the bowl a little to look for that tell-tale jiggle but most often our Jell-O was served with more than one fingerprint on the top.

Gelatin recipes were definitely a staple at every country church gathering. There were at least 15 unique uses for Jell-O from four different decades in Gram's recipe box and it was difficult to narrow down the most interesting and best offerings. If there's one thing that never goes out of style, it's a shiny copper lobster-shaped gelatin mould or the fresh citrusy scent of a bowl of orange Jell-O on a hot summer day.

Horseradish Salad

1 Package Lemon Jell-O
1½ Cups Boiling Water
½ Cup Whipping Cream - whipped stiff
½ Cup Mayonnaise
3 Tablespoons Horseradish - drained

Dissolve Jell-O in the boiling water and allow to cool.

When Jell-O starts to set, add whipped cream, mayonnaise and horseradish. Blend thoroughly and chill until it is set.

I have yet to discover what you would serve this with. Perhaps it's best left to the imagination.

an acceptable level of unemployment, simply means that the government economist to whom it is acceptable, still has a job.

Lime Jell-O Salad

1 Package Lime Jell-O
1 Package Lemon Jell-O
1 Cup Boiling Water
1 Cup Miracle Whip
1 Container Cottage Cheese
1 Large Can Crushed Pineapple with Juice
1 Cup Evaporated Milk
1 Cup Chopped Walnuts

Mix the two boxes of Jell-O with the boiling water. Refrigerate and allow to set slightly.

Into the slightly set Jell-O, beat in the Miracle Whip, cottage cheese, pineapple and evaporated milk.

Refrigerate for a few hours until this is firmly set.

Top with the chopped walnuts.

Tastes just like the '70's!

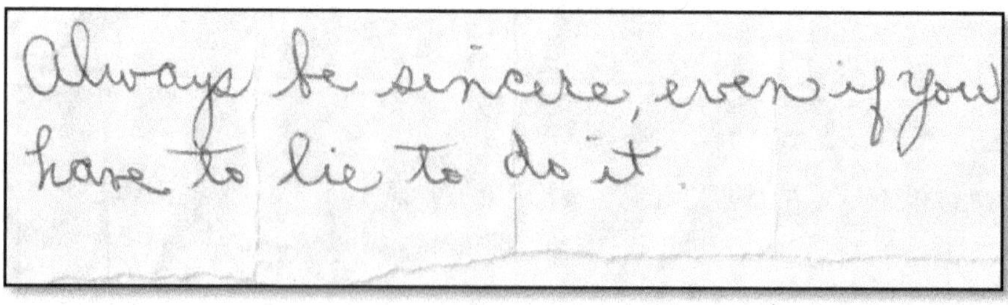

Cabbage Whip

1 Package Lemon Jell-O
½ Teaspoon Salt
1 Cup Boiling Water
½ Cup Cold Water
1 Tablespoon Lemon Juice
½ Cup Mayonnaise (salad dressing)
1 Teaspoon Prepared Mustard
2 Cups Finely Chopped Cabbage
2 Tablespoons Finely Chopped Carrots
2 Tablespoons Finely Chopped Onion
2 Tablespoons Finely Chopped Celery

Dissolve the Jell-O and salt in the boiling water.
Add cold water and lemon juice.

Stir in the mayonnaise and mustard.

Chill until slightly thickened.

Add remaining vegetables and beat with an electric mixer until light and fluffy.

Pour into a greased jelly mould. Let set for 2 hours.

Serves 6

A potluck favourite! (not really)

Layered Orange Gelatin Fluff

1 Package of Orange Jell-O
2 Cups Boiling Water
1 Can Frozen Orange Concentrate (thawed)
1 Cup Cold Water (approximately)
4 Tablespoons Fresh Lemon Juice
½Teaspoon Vanilla
1 Carton Whipped Topping or Whipped Cream

Dissolve the Jell-O in the boiling water.

In a separate bowl, add enough cold water to the orange concentrate to make 2 cups.

Stir orange juice into Jell-O mixture.

Stir in lemon juice and vanilla.

Chill until as thick as unbeaten egg whites.

Measure out 1½ cups of the orange juice mixture into a large mixer bowl and set aside.

Spoon remaining mixture into a serving dish with a 6 cup capacity and chill.

Whip the 1½ cups of orange juice mixture at high speed until light and fluffy and doubled in volume (10 minutes). Pour over top of the chilled mixture.

Chill until set and top with whipped cream.

Like a Creamsicle without the stick!

Coffee Sponge - Great Grandma Millard

This should be made the day before serving.

1 Package Knorr Unflavoured Gelatin
¼ Cup Cold Water
1½ Cup Cold, Strong Coffee
½ Cup Whole Milk
$^1/_3$ + $^1/_3$ Cup Granulated Sugar
¼ Teaspoon Salt
3 Egg Yolks, Slightly Beaten
3 Egg Whites, Beaten Til' Fluffy But Not Stiff
2 Teaspoons Of Vanilla
Sweetened Whipped Cream Or Cool Whip

Soak 1 package of gelatin in ¼ cold water for ½hour.
Mix strong coffee, milk and $^1/_3$ cup of sugar together and add to the gelatin mixture.
Pour into a double boiler and heat
When fully heated (do not boil), add remaining white sugar and egg yolks.
Cook until mixture thickens slightly.
Remove from heat and add beaten egg whites and vanilla.
Pour into individual serving dishes and chill.
Serve cold topped with whipped cream.

This is a secret family recipe, so keep it between us, okay?
Coffee Sponge was a big treat as dessert at Christmas dinner and kept the children very alert for hours.

Chapter Seven

How zippy do you want it?

Farm life was considerably different from city life in many ways. It was definitely a lot more work. I rarely remember Gram just sitting still and doing nothing.

Every minute of her day had a purpose. Multitasking wasn't a trendy catchphrase, it was a necessity. Oddly enough, I never heard her complain or brag about being "so busy" as we tend to do today. If anyone has a right to, it's a farm wife. For my Gram this was just her life.

You didn't squander your resources and your most precious resource is time. At that time, her career was farm operations. She may not have been milking the cows but she kept things running behind the scenes. I'm told that the term "farm hers" is a more relevant option for what my Gram did. I think she'd appreciate that reference.

As soon as the table was cleared and the breakfast dishes were washed, dried and put away, preparations began for lunch. Farm lunches and city lunches are opposite. On the farm, your mid-day meal was a full-on stuff-yourself-to-the-gills food fest to keep you energized for the heavy and often hot work the afternoon would bring.

I try to imagine the look on Poppa Sid's face if he had sat down to a lunch of a roasted beet salad and sliced apples. His first question to Gram would be, "Grace, where's the meat?" Lunch was not something to be trifled with. And you certainly didn't get fancy with the menu.

Gram always had a plan of action. She wasn't a "fly by the seat of her pants" kind of gal. When you are miles from the closest grocer and your husband has the only vehicle, you quickly learn to be self-sufficient.

The freezer was always full of meat and vegetables. They raised the cows they slaughtered. I remember more than one trip to the abattoir and using a rubber stamp to stamp the word "hamburger" on paper wrapped packages. Especially challenging was knowing that a few weeks prior I may have been feeding that same cow some grass in the barn. I learned early on not to get attached to the food source, no matter how beautiful its big, brown eyes were. It definitely made the "What did you do on March Break" assignments more interesting when I returned to school.

Lunch would always have a meat component like roast beef, chicken or pork chops. It would be accompanied by a starch, usually potatoes and a vegetable that had previously grown in Gram's marvellous garden or came from a surrounding farm.

There would be freshly made biscuits or sliced bread. Dinner rolls were served at lunch time too. Butter, not that new-fangled margarine, rested in the flying saucer butter dish. Salt and pepper sat in the middle of the table but wasn't used very often. Gram had a knack for seasoning.

Looking back, Gram's spice cupboard didn't contain much variety. Salt and pepper, onion flakes, cloves, cinnamon, allspice and nutmeg. The most exotic flavour may have been minced dried garlic. It certainly didn't have the world flavours that sit primarily unused in our spice racks today.

Less was more and fresh was best. Chopped onion was all the pizzazz locally grown fare really required. Not to mention knowing how to cook everything to perfection after years of expertise in the kitchen.

Chili

2 Green Peppers Chopped
2 Large Onions Chopped
2 Tablespoons Vegetable Oil
2 Pounds Ground Beef
1 Can Tomato Soup
½ Cup Ketchup
1 Can Beans In Tomato Sauce
1 Can Kidney Beans
1 Can Pinto Beans
¼ Teaspoon Salt
¼ Teaspoon Pepper
½ Teaspoon Chili Powder
¼ Teaspoon Cayenne Pepper
In a large Dutch oven, sauté green pepper and onion in oil.
Add the beef and cook thoroughly. Drain off any fat.
Add the remainder of ingredients and stir.
Allow to simmer for ½ hour.
Serves 6-8 People

Grandma's Note: *You can serve this over cooked spaghetti or macaroni and topped with grated cheddar cheese. P.S. You might like it more zippy - if so add a little more chili powder and cayenne pepper.*

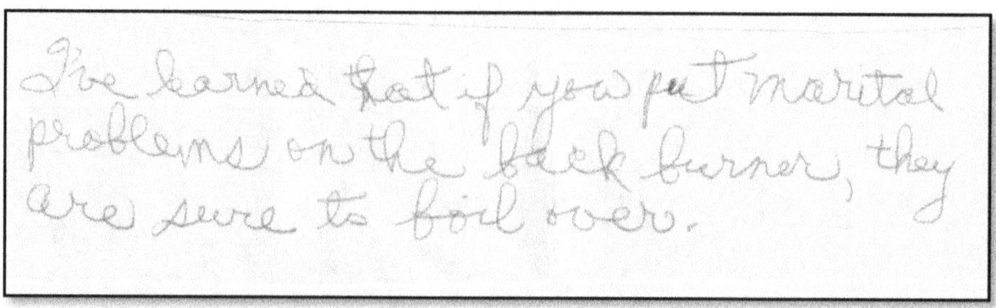

Squash Puff

5 Cups Of Squash, Cooked And Mashed
½ Cup Chopped Onion
2 Tablespoons Butter
2 Large Egg Yolks, Beaten
2 Large Egg Whites, Beaten
¼Cup Milk
2 Tablespoons Flour
½Teaspoon Baking Powder
½Cup Buttered Bread Crumbs
Salt And Pepper To Taste

Preheat oven to 375°.

Sauté onion in butter until clear but not brown.

In a large bowl, mix together squash and onion.

Beat in egg yolks until smooth.

In a separate bowl, mix together flour, baking powder and salt and pepper.

Stir in flour mixture into the squash mixture.

Fold in beaten egg whites.

Pour everything into a buttered casserole dish. Top with buttered crumbs.

Bake for 30 minutes.

Shepherd's Pie

2lbs Lean Ground Beef
1 Tin Mushroom Soup
$^3/_4$ Teaspoon Salt
2 Diced Carrots
1 Cup Diced Onion
1 Tin Tomato Soup
1 Cup Water
¼Teaspoon Pepper
1 Cup Green Beans (Fresh Or Frozen)
2 Cups Grated Cheddar Cheese
3-4 Cups Seasoned Mashed Potatoes

Preheat oven to 350°.

In a large skillet, brown beef and onions. Drain off fat. Add soups, salt and pepper, water, carrots and beans and mix well.

Pour mixture into a large casserole dish. Top with mashed potatoes.

Bake for 50 minutes. Remove from oven and top with cheese.

Serves four to six

Junk is something you need the day after you throw it away.

Tuna And Macaroni Casserole

1 Cup Macaroni, Cooked Until Tender
1 Tin Mushroom Soup
½ Cup Milk
1 Tin Tuna Or Salmon
$^1/_3$ Cup Onion, Finely Chopped
¼ Teaspoon Paprika
Salt And Pepper To Taste

Preheat oven to 350°.

Mix milk, soup, onion until creamy.

Add in macaroni and tuna, salt and pepper.

Pour into a casserole dish. Sprinkle paprika over the top.

Bake for 45 minutes.

Serves four

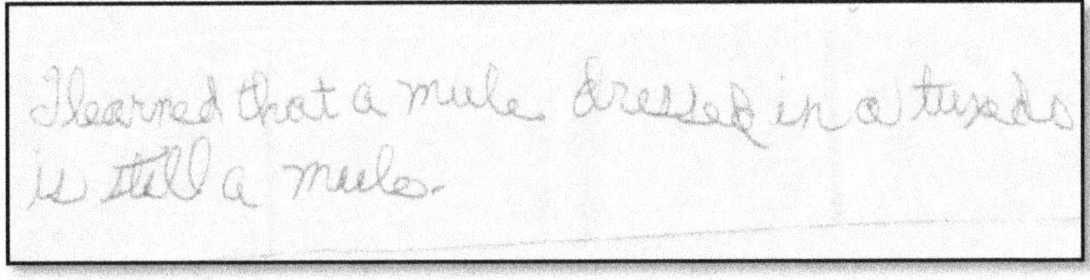

Baking Powder Biscuits

2 + ¼ Cups Sifted All Purpose Flour
¾ Teaspoon Salt
3 Teaspoons Baking Powder
4-6 Tablespoons Shortening
¾ Cup Milk

Preheat oven to 350°

Measure and sift together in a bowl all of the dry ingredients. Add shortening and work into dry ingredients with a pastry blender or hands until the mixture is crumbly.

Add milk a little at a time and stir with a fork until a soft dough is formed (about 20 strokes). You may not need all of the milk.

On a lightly floured board, knead the dough about 20 turns. The dough will be soft but not sticky.

Roll the dough to about ½ inch in thickness and cut into desired shape.

Bake on a lightly greased cookie sheet for 12 to 15 minutes.

Grandma's Note: *This is a very versatile recipe. This is a great topping for chicken pot pie. Brush biscuits with melted butter, sugar and cinnamon before baking and use as a base for strawberry shortcake. Top with berries and whipped cream.*

When the summer heat fell on the farm like a Hudson Bay blanket, lunchtime meals didn't waiver. Dinners however, would reflect the afternoon temperatures. I don't remember the farmhouse having central air, just box fans that allowed you to perfect your robot voice impression until Gram shooed you outside.

After baking and cooking all morning, supper was often a cold plate. Today we call them charcuterie and eat them off slabs of live edge wood and pay exorbitant amounts of money for the privilege. Back then, she just called it a "summer supper".

Cold meats, usually sliced black forest ham brought home fresh from Maedels. Small, square slices of old cheddar cheese. Radishes pulled from the garden and cut into roses, swelling in cold water. Sliced cucumber soaking in vinegar. Peeled, sliced and salted tomatoes. Bread and butter pickles I would have fetched from the creepy, dark storage cellar in the basement. If there were any leftover potatoes from the weeks' lunches, a potato salad with crunchy bits of yellow onion and celery would round out the plate.

As convenience and availability of products increased, tuna macaroni salad became a weekly summer mainstay. And the perennial "fruit salad with the marshmallows", still my absolute favourite taste of summer, second only to fresh sweet corn on the cob with salt and lots of melted butter.

There were never any shortages of cold salads to be concocted, usually from traditional recipes handed down from mothers and grandmothers and generally involving a variety of beans. The hilarity that ensues from a family eating a large quantity of beans together can never be underestimated. Thankfully we were on a farm with 50 acres of open space. The threat of a methane explosion was significantly reduced, and the lingering scent could easily be blamed on the livestock or a coincidental manure spread.

I have decided that this tradition can and will end with me, having never enjoyed a cold bean salad that made me want to ask for a recipe, let alone share the after-effects.

Fruit Cocktail Salad

1 19oz Can Fruit Cocktail, Strained
1 19oz Can Pineapple Chunks, Strained
1 Package Miniature Coloured Marshmallows
1 Package Unsweetened Coconut, Finely Cut
1 Pint Sour Cream

Mix all of the ingredients together well in a large bowl.

Refrigerate at least 12 hours before serving.

Great Grandma Millard's Oatmeal and Gingerbread Cookies recipes.

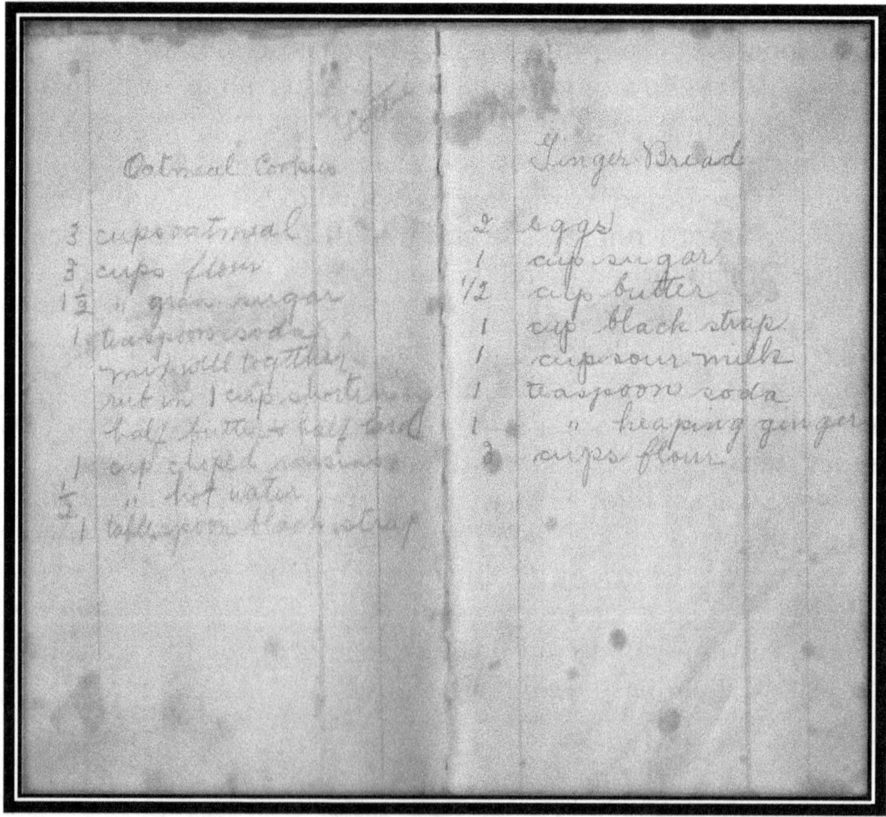

Canada - A Special Person
Grace Roberts - (date unknown)

I am Wayne Gretzky, streaking across the ice in a hockey arena, eyes burning with a desire to excel.

I am the late Foster Hewitt, bringing the first play-by-play hockey telecast over the airwaves and into the homes of Canadians.

I am wheat, spreading rich and gold across the Prairies in late August.

I am Steve Fonyo and Terry Fox, risking their lives as they hobble on one good leg across Canada to raise money for cancer research.

I am a small town girl named Anne Murray from Springhill, Nova Scotia singing "You Needed Me."

I am Marc Garneau, the very first Canadian astronaut to experience flight in space.

I am Billy Bishop and Buzz Beurling and thousands more who fought in wars, those who came back and those who didn't.

I am Don Harron in a tweedy old cap over a whiskery face, making Charlie Farquharson come to life and adding some humour to our lives.

I am the tough memories of the Great Depression.

I am E.P. Taylor and a grade 12 kid looking for a summer job.

I am Charles Templeton and Pierre Berton, bouncing words off each other in lively debate.

I am a Ting cartoon.

I am a walk along the St. Lawrence River by the Plains of Abraham.

I am an Alberta rancher, an Ontario farmer, a Dofasco steel man and a miner from Timmins.

I am a senior citizen on a bus trip.

I am the majestic Rocky Mountains towering over the little town of Banff.

I am Banting and Best's insulin.

I am the rugged shores of Newfoundland, where the fishing boats put out to sea, just as they have for the last 300 years.

I am the Agawa Canyon and the Gaspé in all the splendor of autumn.

I am the winter when the snow piles up to your knees and the cold wind takes your breath away and you think spring will never come.

I am the glorious spring that eventually follows the cold winter, bringing a renewal of life to all things.

I am a lazy summer day in P.E.I. where the good red earth and the sweet smell of clover are all about.

I am a doctor named Dafoe who brought the country's most famous quintuplets into the world.

I am Maclean's magazine, the R.C.M.P., the CN Tower, Calgary Stampede and Ottawa in tulip time.

I am Vancouver Stanley Park on a day that only God could have created.

I am all the church ladies in all the little country churches taking their bows after serving a turkey supper or a wedding dinner, still in their aprons.

I am John Drapeau, Stanley Knowles, Expo '86, Tommy Hunter, Harold Ballard and the Montreal Canadiens.

I am the son of an Italian tailor who for over 50 years brought us the "sweetest music this side of Heaven" as Guy Lombardo and the Royal Canadians.

I am the minister who came from the far-away Philippines and found a home in rural Ontario.

I am the Fathers of Confederation who over a century ago molded this beautiful land into one great country.

I am the Indigenous and the Inuit who have been here longer than memory.

Yes, I am all of this and ever so much more.

I am Canada and I am a very special person. When I stand straight and tall to sing O Canada, if you should see a little tear trickle down my cheek, it's because I'm proud to be a Canadian and I hope you are too.

Chapter Eight

Monsters and Mustard Pickles

Let's circle back to that creepy, dark storage cellar in the basement. You'd be hard pressed to find a farmhouse of old that wasn't equipped with a cold room to store the fall harvest. It was just as important as the kitchen because its contents would sustain the family over the winter and would bring the heebie jeebies to any citified granddaughter. A cellar had to have certain criteria and Gram's hit every single one.

The cellar was of course unseen by guests, yet discussed with great pride. It wasn't so cold as to freeze the bushels of apples and burlap bags of potatoes or burst the jars of preserves. And it wasn't so far away that it wasn't convenient to yell to the kid upstairs in the bedroom to descend two floors to grab a jar of mustard pickles.

The cellar contained wooden shelves where spiders could lurk and watch between the jars of peaches and pears. The wood wasn't new but reclaimed from some other project long forgotten. Some boards were painted, some were not.

The light was a bare 25 watt bulb with a long piece of string attached to the pulley. The bulb flickered a moment before you could step down to the required earthen floor. In that momentary flicker, you could hear four ghastly monsters snarling, their knuckles scraping along the floor coming for you from each corner of the cellar. I knew they were there, but they disappeared the moment the light became fully illuminated.

The earthen floor wasn't the rich brown hue of the garden but a sad, light grey dust that barely moved on impact. No longer the soil used to grow the food but now protecting the harvest in a less theatrical way.

The shelves were full of assorted pint and quart-sized jars of everything and anything grown in the garden. Pickles, peaches and pears, oh my! Applesauce and stewed rhubarb. Plums, cherries, corn, beets and relishes of all kinds. An array of colours that reflected against the glow of the dull light bulb.

Along the wall would rest the crocks used for pickles. I remember what a mystery that seemed to be. Forbidden to open the lid, we just had to believe that the prickly little cucumbers and vinegar dumped unceremoniously into that jar would magically be transformed into the pickles we would eat later on at Christmas.

Never was my endurance tested more than when reaching up to pull the string to turn out that light, arms full of jars, racing up the steps back into the kitchen before the monsters could leave their corners again.

The author kicking back and living the farm life, 1968

Chili Sauce

12 Cups Peeled Ripe Tomatoes (About A 4 Quart Basket)
3 Cups Finely Chopped Celery
2 Cups Chopped Onions
¼ Cup Pickling Salt
2 Cups Granulated Sugar
1 Cup Cider Vinegar
2 Tablespoons Mustard Seed
$1/_8$ Teaspoon Cayenne Pepper
1 Medium Green Or Red Pepper Chopped Finely
1 Small Can Tomato Paste

Pour boiling water over tomatoes to blanch so the skins will peel off easily.

Peel and cut tomatoes into small pieces. Measure into a large bowl and be sure you have 12 cups.

 Stir in chopped celery and onion.

Sprinkle the pickling salt over the tomato mixture and let it stand overnight.

In the morning, pour off excess liquid using a colander, but don't press it!

Pour mixture into a very large pot and add sugar, vinegar, mustard seed and cayenne.

Boil slowly for 45 minutes or until the celery and tomatoes are cooked. Stir frequently!

Add tomato paste and chopped pepper and boil 15 to 30 minutes longer or until pepper is tender.

Pour sauce into sterilized jars and seal using a hot water bath process (jars submerged under boiling hot water for 20 minutes. The lid should not flex up and down when pressed.)

Grandma's Note: *I always use a small bit of chili pepper because I like it zippy. Grandma Millard used a teaspoon of celery seed in her chili sauce, taste and see.*

Heard in an elevator — We're enlarging our apartment next spring. We're scraping off the wall paper.

Hot Dog Relish

1 Six Quart Basket Of Fairly Large Cucumbers
3 Large Onions
¼ Cup Pickling Salt
6-8 Cups Cold Water
1 Tablespoon Celery Seed
4-6 Cups Cider Vinegar
1 Tablespoon Mustard Seed
½ Tablespoon Dry Mustard
4 Drops Green Food Colouring
2-½ Cups Granulated Sugar
1 Medium Sweet Red Pepper Chopped Finely
1 Medium Sweet Green Pepper Chopped Finely
¼ Cup Flour
1 Teaspoon Turmeric

Chop or grind cucumbers and onions. Put into a large bowl and add water to cover. Stir in pickling salt.

Let stand covered at least 3 hours or overnight.

Drain well and place in a large kettle.

Add enough cider vinegar to barely cover the mixture.

In a small amount of cider vinegar mix together celery seed, mustard seed and dry mustard. Add in to the cucumber and vinegar mixture and stir well.

Cook ½ to ¾ hours.

Add food colouring, sugar and peppers. Continue cooking and stir often so that it doesn't stick.

Mix flour and turmeric with a little vinegar and make a paste. Add a little of the hot mixture to it so that it is fairly runny.

Add this flour mixture to the cucumber and cook until thick. Stir often to prevent sticking.

Pour into sterilized jars and seal using a hot water bath process (jars submerged under boiling hot water for 20 minutes. The lid should not flex up and down when pressed.)

Grandma's Note: *When I made this I chopped it up but the next time I will grind up the cucumber. The peppers are better cut up into small pieces. This is your great, great Aunt Lettie Harrison's recipe.*

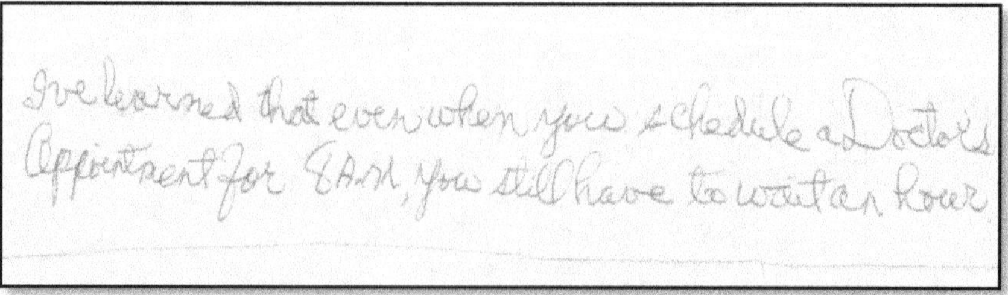

Chapter Nine

The Basement (Less Creepy than the Cellar)

The smell of the cellar was something that has never left my memory. A dark yet comforting reminder that hard work has its own rewards.

Next to the cellar was the laundry room. This was a fascinating museum of days gone past, yet at the time still very much a functioning workspace.

In my city house, we had an electric washing machine and dryer. Gram still used her ringer washer. Why? Because it still worked just fine and cleaned Poppa Sid's dirty butcher aprons better than anything else.

A yellow hard bar of laundry soap sat on the tubs' little stand. Gram would scrub at the difficult stains and plop the article of clothing into the bubbly concoction of swirling fabrics and hot water. Piece by piece, she would pull them up and crank them through the two rollers to wring out the water. She would rinse and repeat until each article of clothing was in a damp pile in the laundry basket.

Watching her also came with warnings not to put my hands near the ringer rollers as they could pull my arms completely off! I believed her but always kind of wondered how she knew this was a possibility. Did it come with a black and white picto-o-gram of someone getting their arms pulled off when tragically trying to dislodge some underpants? Or was this actual farm wife folklore? I'll never know for certain, but I do have two working and attached limbs today since I heeded her warning.

Once the laundry basket was full of damp, clean clothes, we'd head up the stairs and out to the back step where the clothesline was waiting. Item after item, wooden clothes peg after clothes peg, each item was hung to flap and dry in the country air. Poppa Sid's long johns happily dancing in the breeze, each leg kicking like a chorus girl. There were no neighbours to gawk at my grandpa's gitch, so only the mail carrier who delivered the mail from his car window may have had the pleasure of the view.

The sound of sheets snapping in the wind on a clothesline is a comforting one. Running between the sheets, playing made-up games of hide and seek or mystery tunnels would keep us busy for hours. However, the smell of clean, crisp bed sheets that were dried in the country air is like no fabric softener created. A combination of sun, fresh air and cotton snuggled up near my nose is a flashback reminder again that hard work has its own simple rewards.

So many neighbourhoods have bans on clotheslines in the city. It's not esthetically pleasing to some I suppose. I can't think of another symbol of devotion than a load of clean laundry on the line. It's an effort of love for those who own the clothes and for the environment. For Gram, it wasn't about the environment, it was the way she had always done it and it worked. Eventually, she did come to own a modern washer and dryer, but I'm not sure if she ever felt it did as good a job or that she had any extra spare time on her hands. There was always something to fill its place.

A farmhouse basement is a bit of a museum, at least this was our case. My grandparents were from a generation that didn't throw things away. There were many reasons for that.

My grandparents scraped through the Great Depression. Items owned were always of value because you worked hard to earn them. Whether it was a simple pair of galoshes or a teacup with a small chip out of it, if it is no longer fulfilled its intended role, they would find another use for it. Even if it took a decade or two to do so.

In the city, we put our trash at the curb and it gets picked up and taken away, never to be thought of again. In the country, this was not an option. Waste was not considered the same.

From the rafters, I remember a hanging metal lunchbox with Roy Rogers and Dale Evans on the front. It had seen better days but there it hung, waiting to be repurposed.

There were large aluminum cake tins and platters Empty Crown canning jars in boxes, waiting to be refilled with jellies and jams. A thermos with a checkerboard design sat alone, waiting for another chance of a picnic or an early morning ride on the tractor. Some overcoats and rubber boots of all sizes and colours. A few wooden crates and some old pots and pans.

There wasn't a lot to play with from a kid's perspective, with the exception of one glorious item: a ringer telephone.

On the wall, near the stairs hung a very old wooden ringer phone. You had to pick up the black earpiece, crank the handle a few times and when someone answered, you'd speak into the mouthpiece.

When you cranked the handle, it made a very satisfying ringing sound. It was a step back in time for a kid who had a dial phone not only in the kitchen at her house but in the recreation room.

While Gram would be upstairs busy baking cookies or sewing, I would sneak down to the basement to make my calls.

I would crank that handle on the phone over and over again, just waiting for a mystery voice from a bygone era with a mid-Atlantic accent to whisper "Hello darling. I've been waiting on your call, ever so long." My imagination played out many scenarios with each ring. Secret missions, long-lost relatives from across the seas, each crank of the handle was a new story to tell. I'm not sure if that's the outcome Alexander Graham Bell had envisioned when he patented the telephone a hundred years earlier. That some odd little red-headed girl would be making up stories in a basement on a farm in the country, but I think he'd be pleased with my creativity.

Alas, the ringer phone was only connected to the barn so Gram could easily tell Poppa Sid that dinner was on the table and he should hustle in while it was still hot.

The farmhouse basement was definitely a multi-purpose space. Without trying to sound over dramatic or embellished, it was also the stage for a daily burlesque show.

It's not nearly as scandalous as it sounds. There was no chance Gram would allow Poppa Sid to enter her clean kitchen in his smelly barn clothes. In through the kitchen door he would come and down the basement stairs he would disappear. If you waited long enough and paid very close attention, you would hear his stocking feet coming up the stairs. Then as fast as a hummingbird he would flit from the top step and race through the kitchen in his long underwear and into the bathroom to wash up. That sight always regaled him with shrieks of laughter from the grandkids who pretended to be shocked when they caught that white flash out of the corner of their eyes while they were sitting at the dinner table.

> I've learned that as long as I have my health, older gets better all the time

Crisp Oatmeal Cookies

1 Cup Shortening Or 1 Cup Butter (Or ½ Cup Shortening and ½ Cup Butter)
1-½ Cups Brown Sugar, Packed
1 Egg
1 Teaspoon Salt
1 Cup Flaked Coconut
1-¼ Cups Rolled Oats
1-½ Cups Flour
1 Teaspoon Baking Powder
½ Teaspoon Baking Soda

Preheat oven to 350°.

Cream together the shortening and sugar.

Add in the egg. Beat well.

In a separate bowl, mix together well the salt, coconut oats flour, baking powder and baking soda.

Add the dry ingredient mixture to the creamed sugar mixture.

Roll dough into little balls and place on an ungreased cookie sheet. Flatten each ball with a fork dipped in water. For extra crispy, crunchy cookies, flatten thin.

Bake for 12 minutes and cool on a wire rack before storing.

Grandma's Note: *These freeze well.*

Sweet Maries

½ Cup Crunchy Peanut Butter
½ Cup Brown Sugar
½ Cup Corn Syrup (Light Or Dark)
1 Cup Cheerios™
1 Cup Corn Flakes™
½ Cup Finely Chopped Peanuts
¼ Cup Butter

In a medium-sized saucepan, melt the peanut butter, brown sugar and syrup together. Do not boil.

While mixture is still warm, add the cheerios, corn flakes, nuts and butter.

Mix well.

Press into a 9" x 9" ungreased pan and cool.

Cut into squares when firm.

I've learned that when someone hurts your feelings, its unimportant unless you persist in remembering it.

Chapter Ten

Hanging on by an Apron String

As we continued to clear out the cupboards and drawers of Gram and Poppa Sid's house, the memories often overwhelmed me. I would go outside to the backyard of their home where everything was in full summer bloom. It didn't matter where they lived or how old they became, they always found time to garden.

Standing in the neatly manicured grass, surrounded by lilac trees, bird feeders and perennials they had moved from house to house, I breathed it all in. My eyes flooded with tears and my heart filled with a deepening sense of loss. I wanted to take everything home with me and preserve it until my dying day. I wanted to dig up every flower and tree and replant it in my own backyard and continue that growth they started from seed so many years ago. Mostly, I just didn't want to categorize what was left and compartmentalize my grief into a pile of boxes. Yet here I was. In my ears I could hear my Gram whispering to me, "Sheryl, get over yourself". For a woman who left behind a lifetime of nostalgia, she wasn't big on teary goodbyes and whatnot. Don't get me wrong, she liked a hug and a kiss on the cheek, but she wasn't one of those snuggly grandmothers who bury you in their chest and squeeze you until your last memory is of their lily of the valley perfume before you nearly blackout.

I came across the drawer full of aprons. There must have been 30 different designs and styles, each with an obligatory pocket for a tissue. There were Christmas aprons and flowery aprons. Stained aprons and a few with holes and rips. All with long ties to tie into a perfect bow at the back. I can't even remember Gram not being in the kitchen or doing chores without an apron tied around her waist. It was as much of an accessory as her clip-on earrings or her glasses.

I remembered pulling her aprons around my little waist, wrapping it a few times before securing it good and tight with a knot that would take Gram twenty minutes to untie. She never got cross though. Maybe she appreciated having a minute or two to sit down.

Of course, she sewed every apron. Aprons weren't something you purchased from a Sears catalogue unless it was very fancy and never intended to get dirty or stained. I kept five of them and begrudgingly put the rest in a box for a stranger to use in their own kitchen some day.

Years later, the aprons are still wrapped in tissue paper and stored away for some unknown special reason that I have yet to land on. I've never worn them. I've never even really looked at them again. Maybe one day, if I'm fortunate enough to be a grandma, I'll pull them out and have the patience and time to untie the knots from around the wee waist of my own grandchild.

The fitness craze has gone so far that nowadays there are more bicycles stolen than automobiles

What Is Youth?
Grace Roberts - (date unknown)

Youth is not a time of life it is a state of mind.

*A product of the imagination. A vigor of the emotions a predominance of courage over timidity. An appetite for adventure. Nobody grows old by living a number of years. People grow old when they desert their ideals.**

Years wrinkle the skin, but to give up enthusiasm wrinkles the soul. Worry, self-doubt fear and anxiety these are the culprits that bow the head and break the spirit. Whether 16 or 96, there exists in the heart of every person who loves life - the thrill of a new challenge, the insatiable appetite for what is coming next. You are as young as your faith and as old as your doubts. So long as your heart receives messages from your head that reflect beauty, courage, joy and excitement... you are young.

When your thinking becomes clouded with pessimism and prevents you from taking risks, then you are old. And remember, youth is a gift of nature but old age is a work of art.

**With excerpts from Samuel Ullman*

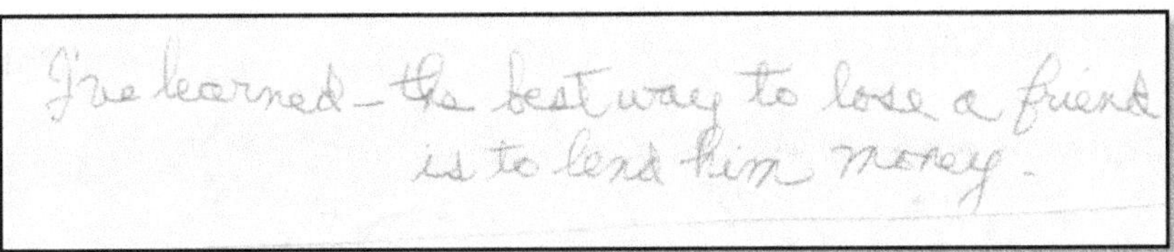

Sauce Pan Brownies

½ Cup Shortening
2 Eggs
4 Tablespoons Butter
4 Tablespoons Cocoa
1 Cup Granulated Sugar
¼ Teaspoon Salt
½ Teaspoon Vanilla
$3/_4$ Cup Flour - Sifted
$3/_4$ Cup Chopped Walnuts Or Pecans

Preheat oven to 325°.

Melt shortening and butter. Add cocoa.
Stir till well blended.

Allow to cool.

Beat in vanilla and sugar. Add eggs one at time, beating well after each.

Add flour and salt to mix. Stir until blended.

Add nuts.

Spread mixture into 9" x 9" cake tin.

Bake for 25 minutes. Do not overbake! These should be soft and almost fudge like.
Allow to cool in the pan on a rack.

Frost when cool.

Grandma's Note: *These are good even without icing!*

Tapioca Pudding 1920's Style

¼ Cup Large Pearl Tapioca
2-½ Cups Whole Milk
2 Eggs
1/3 Cup Granulated Sugar
1/8 Teaspoon Salt
½ Teaspoon Vanilla

Rinse tapioca and soak overnight in cold water.

Drain and add milk.

Cook in double boiler until tapioca is clear (about 1 hour).

In a small bowl, beat eggs. Add sugar and salt.

Pour some of the hot milk over egg mixture and mix well.

Pour the egg mixture into the tapioca and milk. Cook about 5 minutes until it thickens. Remove from heat and add vanilla.

Grandma's Note: *May be served cool or hot with a little jam, cream or fresh fruit.*

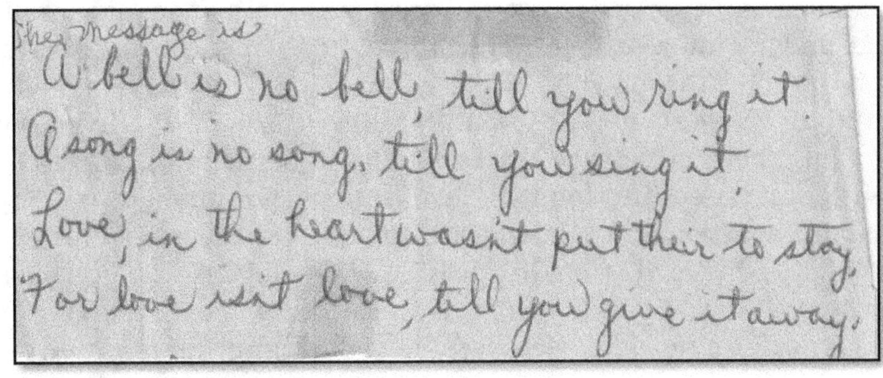

Chapter Eleven

Oh, come, come, come, come
Come to the church in the wildwood
Oh, come to the church in the dale
No spot is so dear to my childhood
As the little brown church in the vale
The Church in The Wildwood, Dr. William S. Pitts

My grandparents rarely missed a Sunday of church once they moved to the farm. After a few years, it was as ingrained in their lives as the sun rising and setting each day. My memories of church with them are limited but always focused on food in some form.

Gram was a member of the church choir at the Newark United Church in Newark, Ontario. She sat at the front of the church with the other choir members as the minister gave his sermon.

I sat with the Poppa Sid on a hard, polished wooden pew. Sunday school hadn't been called yet and at six years old or so, my attention span and my interest in church was limited to about three minutes.

I'd flipped through the black hymn books. I'd reassembled the empty offering envelopes into different patterns in the ledge. Soon enough, I became fidgety. Swinging legs and snapping fingers. This quickly cascaded into loudly whispering observations to my Poppa Sid such as "that man has hair sticking out of his ears" and the ever popular "why is this so BORING?". When all else failed, I could always wave wildly to my Gram who sat there, mortified. The smile was frozen on her face. Her eyes darted around the hundred-year-old church to see if anyone had noticed the little red-headed distraction in the second row.

While the rest of the congregation bowed their head to pray for world peace or some other cause, Gram was sending messages to Poppa Sid using her own kind of frantic sign language and eye rolling. He got the message.

That was the moment my Poppa Sid gave me the ultimate responsibility for a six year old to have. I would be in charge of Gram's purse. Heady times indeed!

He plunked it down on my lap. Its' stiff handle practically touching my nose. Black, heavy and polished patent leather with a brass clasp at the top just begging to be unclasped.

I ran my hands over the clasp about a hundred times until whoops! It opened! How could that have happened?

As if there were a devil on my shoulder, urging me on, I slowly opened the purse. It creaked a little at the hinge, but no one seemed to notice, let alone my Poppa Sid who seemed pretty pleased with himself for having found something to occupy Princess Fidget Pants.

Slowly and ever so discretely, I stuck my hand deep inside. So many shapes and textures at my fingertips! Some items I could recognize right away. A tube of lipstick. A large comb. Her leather wallet. A change purse A handful of tissues - gross!

Amidst all of this sensory overload there was one that heightened the olfactory's. The refreshing smell of mint could not be mistaken in a room that smelled of old books and wet overcoats. This meant only one thing. There was candy to be found! What started out as sentry duty of the purse now had evolved into a delightful scavenger hunt.

You have to keep in mind, my Poppa Sid always had one of two candy options on his person at all times. A variety pack of Life Savers® or Chiclets®. Sweet treats, usually fruit flavoured but consistently welcome to the refined palate of a child. My guess is that he was afraid I would either crunch the candy loudly or chew the gum like a cow with her cud, so it wasn't offered. Regardless, it was the expectation I was used to.

As the choir sang and the minister preached, I fished around every nook and cranny of that bag, pretending to be raising my voice to the Lord, but really worshipping at the feet of Willy Wonka and whatever wonderfulness that was emitting that minty scent.

The long dangly wrapper, it brushed my fingertips ever so lightly. This was it. This was what I had been searching for. I'd found it at last. I clutched the roll in my hand. It wasn't as fat as a roll of Life Savers but when I pulled it out, it had an intriguing, metallic packaging. I handed the pack to my Poppa Sid expectantly. He smiled, took the pack from my hand and whispered "Are you sure you want Grandma's candy?"

There are very few questions posed to a child that are given so little deliberation. They can be answered within a millisecond because the children already know the outcome of their response.

Do you want candy? Yes.

Did you do your homework? Yes.

Do you want me to give you something to cry about? No.

After finally establishing that yes indeed, I surely needed that candy at this point, he peeled back some of the flashy wrapper and handed one to me from the roll. It was a small, opaque disc about the size of a button and smelled delicious.

My Gram, ever observant was watching from her front row seat, that peculiar smile still frozen on her face. I popped that prize into my mouth and rolled it around with my tongue to really appreciate the flavour.

It was very minty and sweet. Soon, however, the sweetness disappeared only to be overwhelmingly replaced with mint. My eyes began to water. My sinuses began to drain. What kind of hellfire was I given, in church of all places?

Poppa Sid leaned over and asked me how I was enjoying my treat. I stuck my tongue out with the offending entity on the tip. I made some strangling sounds and clutched at my throat like I was struggling for air. To anyone not in the know, they may have believed I had been so moved by the Spirit that I was exuberantly praising the sermon being delivered to us. Poppa Sid however knew better. He pulled out his handkerchief and I deposited the candy into it with the power of a cowboy hawking a loogie into a spittoon.

You may be wondering, what was that offending candy? Certs™. High octane, kill-every-germ-causing-bad-breath-in-your-mouth-for- the-next-two-years, Certs. To this day when I taste something extremely minty, I'm rocketed back to that wee country church in Newark and Gram's frozen smile.

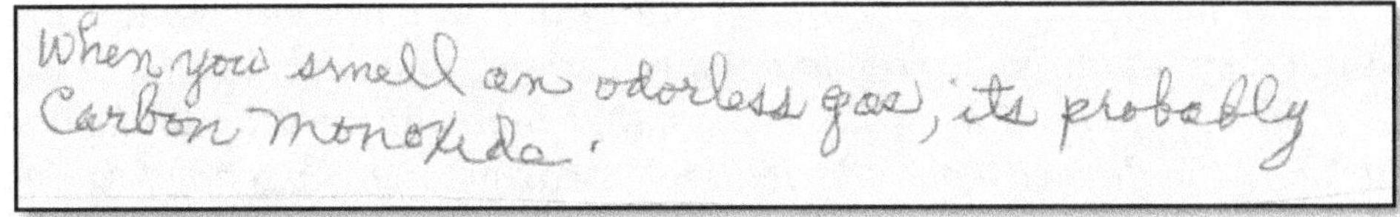

Following church, when the chores were finished and lunch was over, I was allowed to play Gram's piano. After I'd washed my hands of course and showed my hastily dried digits for proof.

It was a very old upright. On the top of the piano were some family photos and a knickknack or two. The keys were ivory and black. Some had a few chips in them from decades of use and misuse. There was a lamp to illuminate the sheet music that had been pulled from the piano bench. The lamp turned on with a snap and warmed the top of my head.

Gram could play well, and she did try to practice often. I would sit beside her on the wooden bench watching her fingers brushing across the keys and her feet tapping the pedals. I was in charge of turning the pages when she nodded her head.

The songs she played most often were hymns. Songs I never knew the words to but listened to intently. Sometimes she would play songs from The Sound of Music and I would sing along while she played.

Her favourite hymn was Church In The Wildwood. I never knew why until I found this piece she wrote tucked away in a scrapbook. This was her church in the wildwood. It was the place of her childhood. How lucky to have a place of comfort and acceptance, and know it from such a young age.

Sheryl Rooth

Profile of a Country Church
Grace Roberts - 1977

Why is it we are sometimes inexorably drawn to a familiar scene from the past, that literally lifts us out of the here and now and drops us unceremoniously into the long ago?

I left our home that beautiful, summer morning several weeks ago to spend the day with an old friend in a nearby town. Instead of taking the main highway as I usually did, some strange magnetic force seemed to draw me down a winding, dusty country road that I hadn't travelled for years.

As I drove along, my mind flooded with memories. It all seemed so familiar. The sharp curves in the little-travelled road, the creaking wooden bridge, too narrow to meet another vehicle, spanning a lazy stream where bushes hung low making a shady refuge for myriads of small creek fish and other aquatic beings.

Slowing to a crawl, I was suddenly aware of the quietness of this place. There was nothing to break the silence but the low, soft tones of a morning dove calling his mate. The hustle and bustle of the world seemed afar off. I felt an undercurrent of expectancy as I continued slowly along, my mind far removed from reality. The road narrowed now and the wheel tracks were barely visible. Wild undergrowth scratched at the sides of the car. As my eyes strayed to the immediate surroundings, I drew in a deep breath and knew instantly what had brought me to this place. There it stood, in what was once a little clearing, almost obscured now by trees and bushes no longer trimmed and tendered.

Wild cucumber vines dripping with morning dew hung from the branches, making a screen that seemed to dare any and all who might intrude upon the privacy of this once-hallowed meeting place, now only a reminder of bygone days.

The country church. How well I knew it. For me and many others it was the place that spiritual growth first took root.

I was overcome with nostalgia as I mused recalling my association with this place. Childhood years and teenage years that had been such an essential part of growing up. Beautiful recollections of Young People's Sunday night get togethers. Crokinole parties, corn roasts, skating parties and all those things the average country kid enjoyed.

I hadn't intended getting out of the car but as I gazed on that rejected, forsaken scene, a strange compulsion came over me and I knew I just had to take a closer look.

The worn, cracked old cement sidewalk leading up to the church was almost grown over with grass and Creeping Charlie. I picked my way gingerly through the maze of cucumber vines and branches until I stood face to face with my own reflection, mirrored in those funny little diamond-shaped pieces of glass in the front door of the entry.

Peering through the glass I could see the door leading to the sanctuary wide open and hanging on rusty hinges. Piles of fallen plaster littered the floor and lacy grotesque cobweb designs dropped from the arched ceiling.

Suddenly I was overcome with a feeling of deep sadness. Could this be the place that once was so alive, so vibrant and vital to this little farm community?

I had at one period in my life thought this church to be indestructible, as firm and everlasting as the Rock of Gibraltar. Now, I was faced with the realization that it was only a building as vulnerable to the changes of time as any other building constructed by human hands.

I walked slowly to the car and as I stood there for a long moment, gazing back, a voice seemed to say to me "Don't be sad. It is not the same as any other building. The spirit of God dwelt within its walls bringing comfort and joy to many generations." How true and beautiful.

This encounter with the past made me think a little deeper about life, about people and about God. It brought happy memories and sad memories, both very much a part of life. It made me realize that God is where we find Him - in a baby's smile, in a woods in springtime, in an elaborate, impressive cathedral or in a country church. Really, what does it take to tune us in to God and the intangible things of the Spirit?

Certainly not a course in theology, or many of us would never know God. It could be a friendly smile from a stranger on the street. A comforting hand on the shoulder in a moment of despair or it could be in times of sorrow or great joy, that God becomes very real. The visit to the country church, which bore the marks as Christ did, of rejection, neglect and complete aloneness, brought me to a new awareness of the need for Christ in my life

In our struggle to keep up with the modern pace let us never forget that we are what the past has made us, that the continuity of life cannot be denied and when we struggle to shake ourselves free of the past we are adding a minus , not a plus to the quality of life.

As I took a last fleeting glance at the old structure, before entering the world of reality. It was like saying good-bye, farewell to a dear friend about to succumb to a terminal illness - for in my heart I knew, I would never pass this way again.

☙

Like many country churches, Newark United was the epicentre for community engagement. Long before community centres and recreation halls became a mainstay the church provided a central location for meetings, activities and socials. It didn't matter how you worshipped God or what your book of rules was, the church was open to all who needed the space.

The church basement was a beehive of activity. For special occasions it would be full of the UCW (United Church Women) laying out the spread of food and coffee percolators. Everyone had their role to play, it was organized and there was no room for nonsense where the food was concerned. That's why the men would be upstairs or outside, staying out of the way, waiting to be called to eat.

If there were no jobs for the children to do, they would be shooed outside and kept from being underfoot of busy women. There was a definite hierarchy in the church if you wanted to eat.

I remember well one occasion where I had been hustled away with the other kids. I didn't know them, as I was really just a visitor most times, but I tagged along anyway. That's the beauty about being a kid, everyone is immediately your pal unless you're told otherwise.

Beside Newark United is the Newark Community Cemetery. It is the resting place for the early pioneers of the area. As one might expect, most children and some adults believe cemeteries to be haunted. I was no hold out to that line of thinking. I held my breath more than once passing a cemetery on the advice of a wise school yard friend who told me this would keep the spirits from sucking away my soul while hiding in the back seat of our car.

The men folk, including Poppa Sid were strolling through the grounds pointing and discussing important grown-up cemetery things. I hesitated to enter, but then all of the other kids were going in too. As a tough city kid, I had a certain reputation to uphold. I couldn't be chicken, especially when all of my new country friends were going in to play.

It didn't matter that I didn't know their names. There was that blonde-haired kid. The boy with the freckles and that girl with the pigtails. All hanging out between the headstones like it was no big deal.

I screwed up my courage and bounded into the grounds acting as though it was very important that I find my Poppa Sid. He was fine of course, but I figured that I was safer that way should zombies or ghosts decide to arrive and try to snatch me away to the underworld.

I walked with the men, sometimes jumping from plot to plot, marvelling at how young or old the people below me were when they died. Despite that natural fear that the decrepit blackened hand of a ghoul would push through the earth and grab me by the ankle at any given moment, I was having a grand time while I waited for my church-lady supper.

There's nothing like a church dinner. Homemade and heartfelt offerings as far as the eye can see. Sitting at one of the long wooden tables and digging in to my dinner, my Gram asked me what I did to entertain myself while she was busy.

Between bites of mashed potatoes and dinner roll, I proudly told her of my courageous visit to the cemetery. Gram stopped eating and put her fork down. Poppa Sid shrunk in his chair a little and suddenly became very interested and focused on his roast chicken.

She pushed her plate forward a little, rested her arms on the table, looked me squarely in the eyes and said "You shouldn't ever play in there. The graves are very old and they could collapse and you'd fall into someone's coffin six feet below the ground. We'd have a difficult time getting you out."

Just like that, she picked up her fork, shot a chilly glance at my Poppa Sid and continued on with her meal, chatting up the lady next to us.

I however, having just overcome a fear of haunted cemeteries, now had a fear of waking the dead by falling into their final resting place because I was goofing around. The hair on the back of my neck stood on end and my soured stomach could only manage one piece of apple pie instead of two. Oh, and a couple of cookies. Plus a brownie. Yes, I was pretty shaken up.

The lesson here? Just sit in the pew with the Good Book and wait for your dinner to be served. You may meet the Holy Spirit but you certainly won't disturb ol' Amos Colborn who passed away in 1850 and miss getting called for supper.

Old Fashioned Chelsea Buns

<u>Dough</u>
½ Cup Whole Or 2% Milk
¼ Cup + 1 Teaspoon Granulated, White Sugar
1 Teaspoon Salt
½ Cup Warm Water
1 Envelope Fast Acting Yeast
1 Egg, Beaten
¼ Cup Shortening
3 Cups All Purpose Flour

Scald milk. Stir in sugar and salt.

Cool mixture to lukewarm.

In a separate bowl, mix sugar into warm water.

Sprinkle the yeast on top of the warm water mixture. Allow to sit for 10 minutes.

In a large mixing bowl with beaters on low, combine the yeast mixture with the milk mixture.

Add the egg and shortening. Beat well.

Beat in 3 cups of the flour until the dough is smooth and elastic.

On a floured surface, turn dough out and knead until smooth. Place dough in a large greased bowl. grease the top of the dough.

Cover the dough and let it rise for 90 minutes or until it has doubled in size.

Punch down. Knead again until smooth.

Halve dough and roll each half into a 9 inch square.

Filling
¼ Cup Butter, Melted
¾ Cup Brown Sugar
2 Teaspoons Cinnamon
½ Cup Seedless Raisins, Soaked In Hot Water And Drained

Mix together the sugar, cinnamon and raisins.

Split the mixture in half.

On each square of dough, brush with the melted butter

Sprinkle the dough with the sugar, cinnamon and raisin mixture

Roll up the dough like a jelly roll.

Cut each roll into about 8 slices

Topping
2 Tablespoons Butter, Melted
½ Cup Brown Sugar
1 Cup Walnuts Or Pecans, Chopped
1 Cup Glazed Or Maraschino Cherries, Halved

Using a two cake pans or 2 9" square pans, pour 1 tablespoon melted butter into each and spread out to cover the entire bottom of the pan.

Sprinkle ¼ cup of brown sugar into each pan.

Sprinkle ½ cup each of nuts and cherries in each pan.

Place the rolls, cut side up in each pan.

Cover and let rise until doubled in size (about ½ hour).

Preheat oven to 375°.

Once rolls are doubled in size, bake at 375° for about 25 minutes.

Allow to cool on a wire rack for 10 minutes.

Turn the pans upside down onto a platter so that the cherries and nuts are on top.

Serve warm.

Grandma Note: *These are very delicious. I used this recipe many times.*

Our life is a book of chapters three,
The past, the present and the yet to be,
The past is gone, it is stowed away,
The present we live with every day.
The future is not for us to see,
It is locked away, & God holds the Key

Angel Cake

1-¹/₈ Cups Sifted Pastry Flour (Sifted 5 Times - Always Sift Flour Before Measuring)
1-¾ Cups Sifted Granulated Sugar (Sifted 5 Times)
1-½ Cups Egg Whites (Approximately 10-12 Eggs)
½ Teaspoon Salt
1-½ Teaspoon Cream Of Tartar
1 Teaspoon Vanilla Or Almond Extract

Preheat oven to 375°.

Sift flour and sugar together into a bowl.

In a large bowl, beat egg whites and sale until foamy.

Beat in cream of tartar. Continue beating until egg whites are standing in stiff peaks. Blend in the extract.

Sprinkle in the sifted dry ingredients (flour and sugar).

Evenly and quickly, fold the dry ingredients into egg white mixture. Do not beat!

Scrape bowl as you pour the mixture into a 10" ungreased tube pan. Cut through several times with a knife to release any trapped air bubbles.

Bake for 30-35 minutes or until golden brown.

Turn cake upside down on a rack after baking to cool.

To make this recipe a chocolate angel cake, substitute ¼ cup of flour for ¼ cocoa and add it to the flour/sugar mixture.

The End of an Outhouse
Grace Roberts - September 1978

In the days of small country stores, rural cheese factories and blacksmith shops, Newark was a thriving western Ontario village. In 1874, its early settlers formed a Methodist Episcopal church.

Nothing is left now of the once bustling village but its little red brick wayside church. To the passerby, the church must give the appearance of quiet serenity, standing quite alone its neat yard surrounded only by fields of corn. No sound breaks the peaceful solitude, save for the whispering pines that line the fence at the rear of the church.

But inside, this is the focal point of the community. The basement is used for many community and church affairs, where people of differing ethnic backgrounds and religions come together in a spirit of community.

Until now, the church has never had indoor plumbing. Many were the trials and tribulations that accompanied the inconvenience of an outdoor facility. Memories of evicting groundhogs and of the icy cold winter, were shared by many who from time to time were caught in an "I gotta go" situation.

At last year's annual meeting, a brave soul among Newark's 50 families spoke up, suggesting a dire need for washrooms and added space for the ever-increasing Sunday school. Some older members could scarcely believe their ears. Only a dozen years ago, Newark church was nearly closed down.

When a vote was taken, a majority were in favour of adding to the church building. Everyone according to their time and talents, worked towards the goal of the new class and meeting rooms and washrooms. The contractors were local people and gave much of their time without pay. The entire community responded to a canvas, bake sales, a walkathon, a dance, spring teas and other activities.

Last fall, on the church's 104th anniversary, the new facilities were dedicated and officially opened.

Agatha's Squares

¼ Cup Butter
½ Cup Peanut Butter
2 Packages Butterscotch Chips
2 Cups Miniature Marshmallows

Melt butter, peanut butter and chips over low heat or in a double boiler over hot water.

Cool to lukewarm. Stir in marshmallows.

Pour into a parchment lined 9" x 9" tray. Allow to cool completely. Cut into squares and store in the refrigerator.

The author (right), her sister Colleen and Mrs. Beasley, in front of Newark United Church, approximately 1975.

Carrot Cake

2 Eggs
¾ Cup Vegetable Oil
1 Cup Brown Sugar, Packed
1-½ Cups Grated Carrot
$^1/_3$ Cups Walnut Pieces
½ Teaspoon Vanilla
1-½ Cups Flour
½ Teaspoon Salt
1 Teaspoon Cinnamon
2 Teaspoons Baking Powder

Preheat oven to 350°.

In a large bowl, beat together the eggs, vegetable oil, vanilla and carrot.

In a separate bowl, mix together the flour, brown sugar, cinnamon, baking powder, walnut pieces and salt until well blended.

Mix the dry ingredients into the egg mixture until well blended and there are no lumps.

Pour into a lightly greased 9 x 9" square cake tin.

Bake for 30 minutes or until a cake tester comes out clean.

Variations:
Add ½ cup crushed pineapple and bake for 40 minutes. Top with your favourite frosting or eat as is.

Decoration Day
Grace Roberts - 1986

Abraham Lincoln once said, "Die when I may, I want it said of me by those who knew me best, that I always plucked a thistle and planted a flower where I thought a flower would grow."

Friends, we are here today not to mourn over the loss of our loved ones who lie buried here but to thank God for their lives and to remember them with joy and thanksgiving for the heritage they have left us.

We must never in any way diminish or lose sight of the continuity of life, that threat that runs from one generation to the next. It is our loved ones who have departed this life who have paved the road we tread, have shaped our lives and our destinies for all time.

All members of the human race have two things in common each of us was born and each of us must die. Most of us are not too concerned with the circumstances of our birth, we don't have any memories of it and it lies far behind us. The thought of dying is quite another matter. The knowledge that our days on this earth will come to an end is an inescapable part of our existence. Sobering, mysterious and sometimes frightening. The thought of death seems to appall some people but under most circumstances it has struck me as a merciful thing. I have talked to doctors and nurses who have seen hundreds of people die and they have told me that the transition from this life to the better life is usually made peacefully and thankfully.

Death is meant to be a friend, not the grim reaper that it has been miscast to be.

We are not here to delve into the mysteries of death, we are here to talk about life. Abundant life. A gift from our creator. From 2 Timothy 1:7, "For God hath not given us the spirit of fear, but of power and of love and of a sound mind."

Life has loveliness to sell.

All beautiful and splendid things.

Blue waves breaking on a cliff. Soaring mountains where a wild bird sings.

Children's faces looking up, holding wonder like a cup.

By dwelling on the anxiety of death we lose our potential to live a full life. As Pope John the 23rd once said "The best way to live is to trust the Lord. To keep peace in your heart. To accept all things as being for the best. To be patient, kind and good. And never do ill.

Hold fast to those words of our Lord.

Peace, I leave with you, my peace to give unto you. Let not your heart be troubled, neither let it be afraid.

I would like to close with this little poem.

"Not until the loom is silent and the shuttles cease to fly. Shall God unfold the canvas and reveal the reasons why. The dark threads are as needful, in the weaver's skillful hand. As the threads of gold and silver in the pattern He has planned."

Lord give me a heart that often sings and finds great joy in little things.

The song of a bird, the smell of a rose
A gentle breeze that playfully blows
A savory meal with loved ones dear
The sound of a church bell, sweet and clear
A mother's love, a child's caress
These are the things that truly bless.

With contributions from Sara Teasdale, poet and Grant Colfax Tullar, composer.

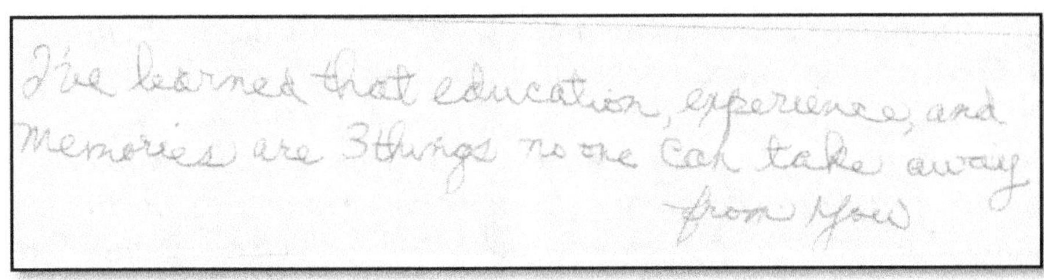

Sheryl Rooth

Grace's Sermon - Mount Elgin United Church - 1983

Smile. God loves you. That probably sounds like a superficial statement but when examined closely, you will see it is a very important part of the impact that we as Christians have in our homes, our community and our world at large. It is the visible way we present our Christian faith to others. If you had an article for sale you wouldn't display the worst features of that article and expect someone to purchase it would you? Are you and I presenting to the world our Christian faith in such a way that others find it irresistible and something they want to be a part of?

Have you ever been out in company where food was being served and getting a morsel of something in your mouth that to you tasted just horrible? You feel that expression on your face is telling everyone exactly how this bite of food tastes to you. By way of comparison, what do you think your expression is telling the world about your Christian faith? Does your countenance tell the world that you have joy and inner peace in our heart because God dwells there? Joy is an intrinsic part of the spiritual life.

In Dr. Leslie Weatherhead's book "That Immortal Sea" he points out that Christians who have no joy in their lives are missing one of the greatest blessings of faith. It is so easy to think negatively these days. Every time we pick up a paper or tune in to the news, we find so many things to be negative about that it overshadows the pleasant and the good aspects of life. Perhaps we could take a lesson from Jesus himself and how he reacted to the evil that was all around him. His country was occupied by an invading army, taxes were exorbitant, hypocrisy and sin existed at a high level among his people. Jesus didn't close his eyes to the evil. He battled with injustice and cruelty to the death. Neither did he let it make him gloomy nor pessimistic. The reason? He had God's promise."Lo, I will be with you always, even unto the ends of the Earth."

How comforting that we also have that promise to us, who are just ordinary people, to know that Christ himself came to Earth as an ordinary person, a carpenter's son. His principal friends were fishermen. He was not a social climber in any sense of the word. He made the ordinary people feel that they had a place in God's kingdom and that they had the capacity to serve Him in many different ways. Jesus talked with housewives, servants and vineyard keepers. No wonder the common people heard him gladly and were anxious to use whatever talent they had to serve him.

The happiest people in the world are those who are doing things for other people. Since coming to Mt. Elgin, I have been impressed with the way people here go out of their way to help others and I've found it to be a happy community.

As long as we are putting others ahead of ourselves, the community will remain happy. It is only when we become engrossed in our own little circle that joy fades from life. Another way we can present our Christian faith to the world is through our vocabulary. Jesus never used language that was disrespectful, sacrilegious. He was not straining to make an impression. On a few occasions I have listened to ministers whose vocabulary was so far above my intellect that I got absolutely nothing out of what they were saying. I imagine you've had that same experience.

From the New Testament scriptures, we read that Jesus talked about birds and flowers and sunsets...of a man plowing in the field... a woman sewing...a shepherd looking after his sheep. All things we can relate to. All through the New Testament we read over and over again of God's love. The message was and is, "I have come that you might have life and that more abundantly". Jesus never put conditions on his love. He never said "I will love you if..." He had love to give, healing to give and teaching to give. And he freely gave them all.

The Lord has never asked us to go anywhere he has not gone, to face anything he has not faced, to love anyone he has not loved, or to give anything he has not given. The gospel picture of Jesus is of a joyous man with a warm sense of humour and a buoyant love of life. New Testament language describes him as anointed with the oil of gladness. There are many passages of scripture about joy, happiness and humour. Jesus could scarcely say enough about joy. Our Christian calling is an invitation to enter into the joy of the Lord.

Joseph Haydn, the composer was once accused by an overly pious critic of writing religious music that lacked seriousness. Haydn straightened his shoulders and answered firmly "Sir, I can compose in no other way. When I think of God, my heart is so full of happiness that the notes run ahead of me. And since God gave me a joyous heart, I think he will forgive me if I serve him joyously."

It makes me think of the old gentleman who seemed to have an unusual amount of trouble and very few pleasures and yet he was always cheerful. When asked the secret of his cheery disposition he replied "Well, you see it's like this. The Bible says often it came to pass, but it never says it came to stay."

I have a little story I would like to tell you called "The Parable of a Water Beetle" which demonstrates the greatness of God's love. The famous motion picture producer Cecil B. De Mille was a man who liked to go off by himself to think out a problem. One time, when he was faced with a vexing personal problem, he went out in a canoe on a lake near his home and spent a whole afternoon quietly drifting, thinking and meditating.

After awhile, the canoe floated inshore where the water was shallow. Looking down he saw the lake bottom was crowded with beetle-like bugs. One of the beetles came to the surface and slowly crawled up the side of the boat. Finally, it reached the top and grasping fast to the wood, it died. Mr. De Mille soon forgot the beetle and went back to his home with worrisome thoughts.

Several hours later, he noticed the beetle again and saw that in the hot sun, it's shell had become very dry and brittle. He watched it slowly split open and there emerged a dragon fly which took to the air out of the old husk, its scintillating colours flashing in the sun. That winged insect flew farther in an instant than the water beetle had crawled in days.

It circled back, swooping down so that it made a shadow on the water. The water beetles below might have seen it too but now their airborne companion was in a world beyond their comprehension. They were still in their limited world while their companion had all the freedom between earth and sky. When telling of his experience later, Mr. De Mille asks a very penetrating question, "If God does that for a water beetle," he asked, "don't you believe he would do this for me?"

God loved the world so much, he gave his only son, that whoever believes in Him shall not perish but have life everlasting. Smile, God loves you. Let us pray. This is the day that the Lord has made, let us rejoice and be glad in it. Let it fill you with love, which is patient and kind. Take away from us all jealousy, rudeness and selfishness. Give us a spirit of gladness which will bring gladness to others. In thy name, amen.

Poppa Sid plowing the fields.

Chapter Twelve

I'll Have The Cocky Crab Apple Pie For One

If you've ever looked for a way to keep children occupied in the kitchen, a flour sifter and an enormous tin of white flour will do the trick every time. Gram had such a tin.

You didn't purchase small amounts of anything that you used often, you bought it in bulk. Flour, sugar, eggs, the staples you used daily and couldn't run to the corner store for.

The flour tin was enormous and held a stainless steel sifter with a red wooden knob on the top of the handle. The knob had been turned so many times that the red paint was wearing thin to a weak pink.

As Gram prepped fillings for pies or cracked eggs to brush over crusts, I would dutifully sift flour over and over again until the particles filled the air and my nose.

It was no surprise that Gram made the airiest bread and the most tender pie crusts. It was all due to the supreme super-sifting power of her grandchildren. To this day, opening a fresh bag of white all-purpose flour and inhaling that rich, cakey scent that takes me back to the tin and sifter so long ago.

There was little that my Gram couldn't bake. Butter tarts cookies, squares, bread and the lightest angel food cakes you ever tasted. The freezer always had treats hidden away behind the frozen orange juice concentrate. They were always wrapped up in waxed paper and tucked neatly into old biscuit and tea tins.

When I was about nine, Gram opened her kitchen to me to attempt my first solo baking challenge. I felt I was ready to surpass Jell-O making, especially considering the exceptional flour sifting abilities I had been carefully honing.

It was harvest time on the farm and time to collect the hay bales from the fields. This was an exciting event. We were allowed to be on the hay wagon as the old John Deere pulled us along, climbing higher and higher as we dodged the bales being tossed up. Swaying back and forth, the hay would scratch and prick our legs, but we didn't care. We scrambled out of the way of the bales, being careful not to fall off.

Along the hay route was the edge of the forest that was on the farm property. The trees were full of crab apples that you could pull from every branch. They were so plentiful you could pick one, take a bite, throw it away and pick another. The sour apples

puckered our cheeks but fit perfectly in the palms of our small hands.

Having many Laura Ingalls Wilder books under my literary belt, I

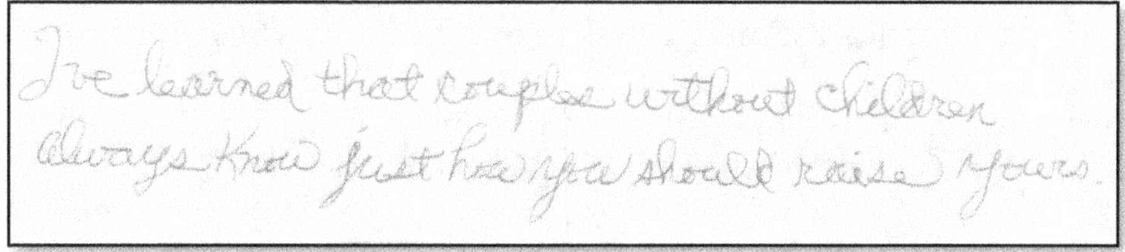

knew that these apples were good for more than a sour bite and a toss. I knew that I could turn these into a delicious apple pie.

I collected as many apples as I could before the tractor pulled us back to the hay rafters of the barn. I nestled the apples as carefully as a dozen eggs between the bales. As we climbed the hill to the top of the barn, I knew my Gram would be pleased with my pioneer spirit and would greet me with open arms to her pristine kitchen where I would in fact create the best crab apple pie in the history of crab apple pie baking.

I carefully walked down the hill from the barn and to the kitchen door with my tiny, ascorbic treasures wrapped up in the bottom of my shirt. I threw open the door in excitement and yelled "Grandma! I'm going to bake you a pie!"

She didn't discourage me, although looking back, I'm sure after a long, hot and busy day the last thing she wanted was a gigantic mess in her kitchen. She handed me an apron and helped me pick over the apples and showed me how to look for wormholes.

"Do you know what's worse than finding a worm in your apple, Sheryl?" she asked me with a knowing smile. I shrugged.

"Half a worm."

Gross!

For a nine-year-old, I will admit I was pretty confident in my kitchen skills. I mean nine years is a long time to watch and learn from a master chef. I didn't need a recipe for pastry. I'd watched Gram make it a hundred times or more. Add in all that sifting training, and I was already ahead of the curve.

How hard could it be to make filling? It's an apple pie, apples need no enhancement, right?

Gram left me to my own devices in her beloved kitchen and went to the living room to relax with Lawrence Welk.

Just as I was creating my pie crust, my Poppa Sid came in from the barn. He looked at me. He looked to my Gram in the living room, stood silent for a moment contemplating his next move and then turned on his heels and went to the basement to change. He knew better I guess, than to interrupt the pie-baking process.

I had my crust ingredients at the ready. The flour, the lard, some water and salt. I spooned, I mixed, I blended and stirred. This goo did not resemble the crust of my Gram. I kept adding flour until everything stopped sticking and became a solid mass. The wooden rolling pin became a jack hammer as I pounded the mass flat enough to fit it in a tiny pie tin.

Now we were cooking!

I cut the crab apples into bite sized chunks, giving extra care to check for sections of worms. Into the crust they went.

It was looking more and more like a pie with every passing minute! I knew Gram used some kind of brown spice so off to the spice cupboard I went. I had my choice of cloves, cinnamon, allspice and nutmeg. All kinds of brown colour but it was hard to know. I figured the best choice was allspice because it was all of the spices. I was a clever girl.

In went a healthy dash of allspice to coat the top of the apples. I was ready to add the top crust to what would no doubt be a blue ribbon winning apple pie.

More pounding with the rolling pin until the last of the now very solid lump of dough was flat for the top of the crust. I cut out two holes with Grams thimble just as she always did, to let the steam escape and then carefully placed the crust on the top.

With much effort, I crimped the edges of the crust together and skillfully cut off the excess dough. I then brushed the crust top with some beaten egg and gingerly placed the pie into the oven. I probably should have preheated the oven but a masterpiece will wait for no temperature.

I looked around the kitchen and contemplated going to watch TV or attempt to clean up what looked like a nuclear testing zone that had been coated in white fallout ash. I decided that cleaning up my mess was probably my only true option, seeing as I had been trusted with such responsibility.

There was no dishwasher. No nifty cleaners or gadgets. Elbow grease would be required. Who knew a countertop coated in flour would not clean up well with a sopping wet dish rag? Clearly not a nine-year-old who loaded a dishwasher every night. Also, wooden rolling pins do not ever need to "soak" overnight, according to Gram.

As I was toiling, the smell of apple pie filled the kitchen. I opened the oven door so often to check on the progress of my 6-inch pie, I added an hour of baking time to the process.

Soon the smell of allspice and apples filled the kitchen. Followed quickly by the overpowering punch-in-the-face smell of burnt allspice filling the kitchen. This sure didn't smell like my Gram's apple pie.

Finally it was time to remove this gastronomic work of art from the oven to cool. It looked like pie, but there was no sweet smell or juices bubbling through the steam holes.

Gram came out to the kitchen to take a look at it and she smiled. Poppa Sid followed quickly behind: he smiled too. I cut into the pie with much effort and smiled at myself. My first pie!

I offered them the first bite, to behold the glory that was this fine dessert. They politely declined, saying it wouldn't be fair to take away even a bite or two from me. After all, it was a teeny, tiny pie.

Secretly, I was relieved. Having a younger sister and brother meant I always had to share everything. My greedy little belly grumbled as I sat at the kitchen table, fork in hand.

I put the fork to my lips and tasted that first bite.

Gram smiled.

Poppa Sid smiled.

I did not smile.

And that was the day that ended with butter brickle ice cream from Shaw's Ice Cream and the crab apple pie in the garbage.

Great Grandma's Raisin Pie

2 Cups Seedless Raisins
2 Cups Boiling Water
1 Tablespoon Water
½ Cup Brown Sugar, Firmly Packed
2 Tablespoons Cornstarch
½ Teaspoon Salt
1 Or 2 Tablespoons Lemon Juice
1 Tablespoon Butter
½ Teaspoon Vanilla
1 Egg, Separated
1 Unbaked Pie Shell With Top

Preheat oven to 375°.

Melt butter and sugar in a saucepan and brown while stirring.

Add boiling water. Add raisins. Let this simmer for ten minutes.

Mix egg yolk, cornstarch and salt in a small bowl with the tablespoon of water.

Stir cornstarch mixture into raisin mixture.

Add lemon juice and vanilla.

Allow this mixture to simmer on low until thickened.

Cool and pour into an unbaked pie shell.

Cover the pie with strips of pastry or a whole top with two holes cut in for ventilation.

Bake for 45 minutes on the centre rack of your oven.

Great Grandma Millard's Vinegar Tarts and Pumpkin Pie recipes.

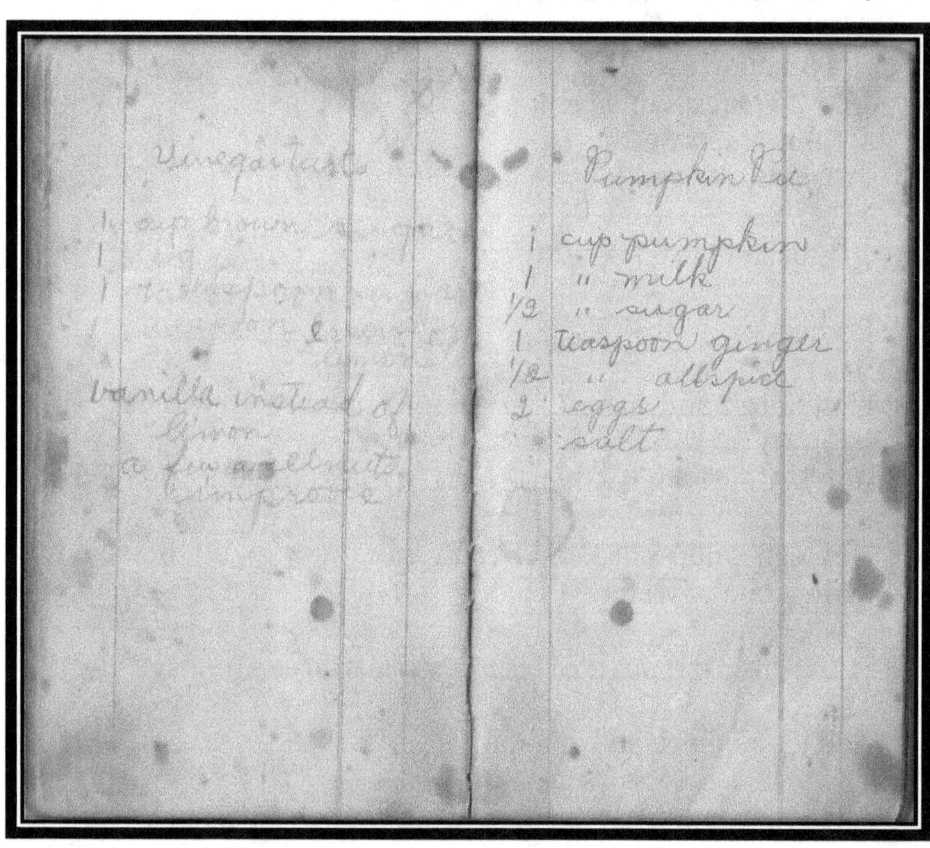

Pumpkin Pie

1-½ Cups Cooked Or Canned Pumpkin (Not Pie Filling)
½ Cup Brown Sugar, Firmly Packed
½ Cup Granulated Sugar
½ Teaspoon Salt
1-¼ Teaspoon Cinnamon
½ Teaspoon Ginger
½ Teaspoon Nutmeg
1 Teaspoon Vanilla
1-½ Cups Homogenized Milk
2 Standard, Unbaked Pie Shells Or 1 Large Pie Shell

Preheat oven to 400°.

Beat eggs in a large bowl for about one minute.

Pour in the remainder of ingredients and blend with an electric beater for two minutes.

Pour into an unbaked pie shell.

Bake for 15-20 minutes at 400°.

Reduce the heat to 350° and bake for another 45 minutes.

The pie is baked when a butter knife inserted comes out clean.

Serve with whipped cream or vanilla ice cream.

Yummy Butter Tarts

½ Cup Light Or Dark Corn Syrup
½ Cup Granulated White Sugar
1 Large Egg
1 Teaspoon Vanilla
Pinch Of Salt
1 Tablespoon Soft Butter
1 Dozen Unbaked Tart Shells

Preheat oven to 350°.

Mix syrup, sugar, egg, vanilla, salt and butter together until well blended.

Spoon mixture into unbaked tart shells.

Bake on the centre rack of your oven for 12-18 minutes until the mixture is bubbling and the shells have crisped.

The minister stood up in front of the congregation + announced, I got some bad news, some good news + again some more bad news for you. The bad news the church roof is leaking + it will cost $15,000 to repair it, the good news is we have the money. The bad news is, its still in your pockets.

Fresh Fruit Pie (Strawberry Or Raspberry)

4 Cups Fresh Berries
¾ Cup Water
3 Tablespoons Cornstarch
1 Cup White Sugar
$^{1}/_{8}$ Teaspoon Salt
1 Teaspoon Lemon Juice
1 Baked 10 Inch Pie Crust

Place 3 cups of whole berries in a baked 10 inch pie crust.

Cut the remaining cup of berries in halves or quarters.

In a saucepan, combine cornstarch, sugar, salt and water until well blended.

Over medium heat, add the remaining cut up berries to the cornstarch mixture and bring the mixture to a boil, stirring constantly.

Reduce to a simmer and cook until thickened.

Cool slightly and add lemon juice.

Pour mixture over berries in the shell.

Place in the refrigerator and chill well.

Serve with whipped cream or ice cream.

For years Gram never shared her recipe with me for her pastry, yet she would always give me grief if I dared to use a frozen pie crust or a mix from a box. My pie crust making never really improved in thirty years and could reasonably be used to shingle a roof. It wasn't until I was nearly 40 years old before she shared with me her secret pie crust recipe.

"There's no secret to good pastry. Follow the recipe on the package of Tenderflake® lard and don't be afraid to get your hands in it" she revealed. I compromise. I buy frozen Tenderflake® pie crusts instead.

Gram's Pie Crust (aka Tenderflake Pie Crust Recipe)

1-¾ Cups All Purpose Flour
¾ Teaspoon Salt
¾ Cup Tenderflake® Lard
4 Tablespoons Cold Water

Mix together flour and salt in a large bowl.

Cut in lard with a pastry cutter or gently with fingertips until mixture resembles coarse oatmeal.

Gradually add enough water to make dough cling together.

Gather into a ball and divide in half. Shape each ball into a flattened round on a lightly floured surface.

Wrap each round in plastic wrap and refrigerate for 30 minutes. Roll out on a lightly floured surface and place in pie tin.

Chapter Thirteen

To Tell The Truth

My grandmother was quite an accomplished seamstress and quilter. She was a master with a needle and thread. When she made quilts, they were always made by hand until her arthritis caused her too much discomfort. Stitch after painstaking stitch, the blanket stretched out on her quilting rack. When she was working on clothing or curtains, her Singer sewing machine was her greatest tool. No new-fangled electric technology in this house. Her machine was powered by a black iron foot pedal that worked the needle. She controlled how quickly the stitches flowed by how fast she pumped her foot. It was a fascinating process, one that every kid would be challenged to resist watching. Or trying.

When I knew Gram was out of earshot, I would race up those polished wood stairs to the second floor landing where her sewing area was. In my haste I would slip and scrape my shins on the edges of the steps while trying not to fall more. By the end of summer my legs would resemble over-ripe bananas from all of the bruises.

I'd listen again for Gram and carefully slide into the seat in front of the machine. I'd put both feet on the pedal and start pumping slowly. I'd watch the needle bob up and down, the thread following along. Oh if only I had some fabric!

My hand brushed the foot plate and I pretended to push material away with the stitches. Faster I pedalled. Faster and faster my feet pushed until a horrible crack was heard.

The pedal stopped. I could no longer see the needle. I could also hear Gram back in the kitchen.

I had two choices. I could slip away from the machine and act like I hadn't been anywhere near it, or I could come clean and tell my Gram the truth. I had mere seconds to make this life-affirming decision.

I went downstairs and ate my lunch like nothing happened. You didn't really think I was going to tell, did you?

A few days later as I was sitting at the piano, not mastering the scales, I heard an "Oh no!" followed by an angry "Sugar!" It came from upstairs. Sugar was the equivalent to the F-word to Gram. She was at the sewing machine and the jig was up.

I went with trepidation to the foot of the stairs and called up "Are you okay, Gram?" I'm sure my voice was as squeaky as a mouse. She didn't respond. I walked up a few steps and could see her trying to untangle a web of thread from her needle and bobbin. It was a knotted mess that could never be unwound.

She grabbed her sewing shears and started snipping away the strands. She glanced at me standing halfway up the stairs but said nothing.

Without her saying a word, I knew she knew. She knew I knew. The look of disappointment on her face was almost unbearable. I said I was sorry, and she sent me outside to play. I'm sure at the time I thought I got off easy but to this day, when I come across those antique sewing machines I remember that day like it was yesterday. That look from her was worse than any words or punishment she could have doled out. That was a lesson well learned.

Gram creating one of her many quilts. Note the apron.

Chapter Fourteen

Spuds With A Side-Order of Soft Serve

The vegetable garden hidden behind the tall cedar hedge was a sight to behold. Row upon row of vegetables of all kinds. Beans, tomatoes, corn and radishes and of course many, many hills of new potatoes.

Visiting my grandparents on the farm in spring, meant two things: my birthday and the planting of the potatoes.

I remember racing out of the car and heading out to the barn to see Duffy, the farm dog and whatever new cats had arrived since my last visit. The only thing that would stop me in my tracks was the neat row of burlap sacks that would be full of seed potatoes.

Those sacks meant I would be busy making little hills of dirt and planting stinky old potatoes for what seemed like days. Granted, it was in all likelihood just a few hours, but felt like so much longer in kid-time.

In our bare feet, the cool dark earth between our toes, my siblings and I would plant the little potatoes with their wiggly white eyes in each hill. Our fingernails and toenails became crusted in dirt. What was the exchange for toiling away the hours as an intern farmhand? It was the field trip of the season, a trip to the Tastee Freeze!

The Tastee Freeze was a drive-in ice cream shop that served soft-serve ice cream treats. You have to understand, an excursion like this was a big reward. My grandparents rarely treated themselves this way because in their world all the treats they could ever enjoy were in their cupboards and fridge. Why spend money on an ice cream cone in town when there was a carton of Shaw's ice cream in the freezer?

For us kids, leaving the farm was a rarity. It was exciting to see new faces. Ice cream at the Tastee Freeze was a tremendous incentive to work.

We were never permitted the fancy sundae or banana split offerings. I think the thought of dropping syrups onto his car upholstery was more than Poppa Sid could bear. Nor would Gram be able to clean us up with a spit-moistened tissue pulled out from the depths of her purse.

No, it would be cones for the lot of us. Sometimes we'd get a chocolate and vanilla mixed twisty cone, which really was living the high life. It was a cool and creamy treat that we earned. Maybe that made it taste even more delicious than it already was.

Forty or more years later, I still remember the neon yellow haze of that ice cream shop and the way the ice cream smelled in that fresh, crisp cone. More so, I remember sitting at the dinner table and Gram proudly announcing that the new potatoes we were digging into were the spuds we had started months before. They were so fresh and delicious even without butter or seasoning.

Isn't it interesting how tastes and smells deliver precious memories when you least expect it? I'd trade a thousand twisty cones today however for one bowl of new potatoes from Gram's garden.

Corn And Tomato Chowder

1 Tablespoon Butter
$^1/_3$ Cup Chopped Onion
1 Clove Garlic, Minced
2 Tablespoons Flour
1 Can (19oz) Tomatoes
2 Potatoes, Diced
1 Cup Chicken Stock
2 Cups Milk
2 Cups Corn
Herbs, Salt And Pepper To Taste

In a saucepan, sauté onion and garlic in butter until tender.

Sprinkle flour into saucepan and blend well.

Stir in tomatoes and bring to a boil, stirring often.

Add potatoes and chicken stock. Boil gently until potatoes are tender.

Heat milk until hot but not boiling. Add to the tomato and potato mixture.

Add corn and heat until it is warm all the way through, stirring often. Add seasoning to taste.

One of my great responsibilities on the farm was to keep the birds and animals out of the vegetable garden. Much hard work and patience went in to each row of vegetables and there was no way my Gram was going to be bested by varmints.

Throughout the spring and summer and sometimes if we were blessed with extended summer weather into the fall, I would be used as the human scarecrow.

As you may imagine, I took on the role with vigour. After all, this food was going to last throughout the great winter to come. I should also remind you that those Little House on the Prairie stories may or may not have given me a little trouble in how I could differentiate between the severity of an 1847 winter and a 1977 winter.

There was no set timetable to go out and secure the garden. Looking back, I believe it's likely each time my precocious self was getting on my Gram's last nerve.

My tools were a well used pair of aluminum pie tins and the shrill shriek my voice.

I would begin at the edge of the garden, barefooted and cautious. One must not alert intruders to your presence too quickly as it ruins the element of surprise. I'd crouch down behind the potato plants and wait for the trespasser to appear.

Usually it was birds. Grackles and crows were the worst offenders. They would swoop in with their taunting "Caw! Caw!" I would spring into action, banging my pie tins together scaring them off.

Birds, squirrels, chipmunks and rabbits. It really didn't matter how cute and furry they were, I had a job to do. This was no time to play favourites.

Every opportunity I had to defend the garden from predators was taken. It wasn't quite so much fun in the rain, but Gram was a firm believer that I was not made of sugar and the animals and birds didn't care that it was raining if they were hungry.

As the growing season dragged on, I too grew a little tired of this constant game of cat and mouse. How many times did I have to bang those tins together before these little burglars started to take the hint that this garden wasn't their personal smorgasbord? Shortly before Labour Day was when 'The Incident' happened.

I was in position, pans in hand. Gram was hanging laundry on the line. Every few minutes I could hear the squawk of the pulley over the cedar hedge. The warm morning sun was overhead. Dew was still drying on the grass. I scanned the garden and spotted a landing crow. His black eyes locked with mine. He stretched his wings and cackled his "Caw! Caw!" I stood my ground and smashed those pie tins together and started to run towards the crow.

"Crash! Crash" went the pie tins. My legs picked up steam as I tore through the vegetable plants. That's when the words so easily slipped from my lips in a shout, not a whisper.

"Get out of here you son of a bitch!"

The crow flew away into the sun.

I turned triumphantly to see Gram at the edge of the garden with her hands on her hips, her apron flapping in the breeze. She did not have on a happy face.

"Sheryl! What did you just say?" she asked incredulously.

I repeated what I had said. (It's never fair that we ask children to repeat a swear word and still give them trouble for swearing!) I was then frog-marched back to the house and given a stern talking to about what words ladies should choose when expressing themselves. Boy! Was she ever cross! I didn't hear Gram swear until she was ninety years-old when my sister and brother and I dared her to do it. I guess at that age she felt she had nothing to lose and no one left to impress.

I can't say my vocabulary ever returned to being so chaste after the garden incident, but I learned very quickly what was and was not appropriate for Gram's delicate ears. Even if another soul couldn't hear me for miles and miles.

Chapter Fifteen

Soda Squints

The first thing my dad would do when we arrived on the farm would be to pour himself a glass of cold water from the kitchen tap. He would drink it all down at once and sometimes get another. I never understood why he was so thirsty by the time we'd arrive at the farm from London. After all, we didn't travel there by covered wagon. He wasn't leading a team of horses through the fields and streams. We had an Oldsmobile!

When I finally asked why, he said, "It's well water. It just tastes better." Truth be told, I couldn't discern the subtle nuances of city water, well water or toilet water for that matter. I do know that what made my water taste best was when Gram pulled out the Freshie packets. Freshie was the Canadian equivalent of Kool Aid. No smiling pitcher crashing through brick walls for this country. We had the quintessential Canadian bird, the toucan.

Gram would reach into the cupboard and pull out four or five different flavours to choose from. The smiling toucan on the packet was a trusted friend. It was difficult to choose from so many delicious options. Lemon-lime, tropical punch, each one more vibrant in colour than the last, each guaranteeing a taste sensation and a pretty impressive matching moustache and tongue right from

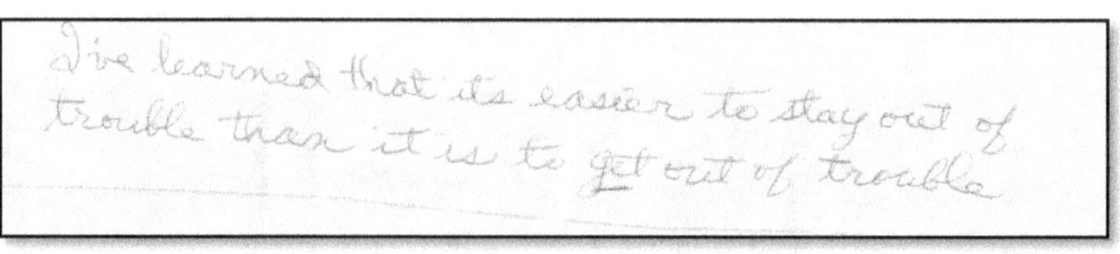

the first big gulp.

Once the decision was made my Gram would fill a large pitcher with water. Slowly I'd pour in the sugar and the packet of flavouring, watching that Technicolor tornado swirl until they were dissolved. A tall glass of Freshie on a hot day was a welcomed treat. Our red and green mustaches that never wiped off were a constant source of irritation to Gram, especially if we were going to be seen in public. What would the customers at Towers think?

Equally as tasty was the rare treat of a half glass of Wink, a grapefruit-flavoured pop that we were given at Christmas. It was tart enough to make you squint on the first sip. It was bubbly and acidic and I felt very grown-up to have this over ice, in a glass trimmed with gold.

I had two choices: slurp down quickly that sweet nectar of the gods and hope there would be a second offering (there never was) or nurse it like I'd never taste it again in my lifetime.

Lacking impulse control, I would slurp it down, my eyes watering, burping quietly so as not to let Gram know my choice. I'd let the ice cubes melt so that any drips of Wink remaining in that fancy glass would meld together to become a second drink. More of a mouthful than a drink of course, but you see my resourcefulness. My only other alternative was well-water and that wasn't quite the same thing, no matter how hard my dad tried to sell it.

I've learned it doesn't cost anything to be nice

Kapok Tree Punch

2 Oz Unsweetened Orange Juice
2 Oz Pineapple Juice
2 Oz Lime Juice
1 Oz White Rum
1 Oz Amber Rum
1 Oz Dark Rum
¾Oz Grenadine
1 Teaspoon White Sugar
Orange Slices And Maraschino Cherries

Combine juices, sugar and white and amber rums.

Shake well. Pour into a tall glass, half-filled with crushed ice.

Top with grenadine and dark rum.

Garnish with an orange slice and a cherry.

I've learned that if you laugh & drink soda pop at the same time, it will come out of your nose

Non-Alcoholic Sangria

1 Quart Of Orange Juice
3 Quarts Non-Alcoholic Dry Red Wine
2 Oranges Washed And Sliced
1 Lemon Washed And Sliced
1 Cup Grapes Washed and Cut in Half
1 Cup Fresh Cherries Washed, Pitted and Cut in Half
Up To ¾ Cup Confectioner's Sugar (Optional)
Soda Water (Optional)

Mix together all except the optional ingredients in several large pitchers and let stand for 4 to 6 hours.

Add ice and taste. If you wish it sweeter, stir in sugar to taste. If you like it a little lighter, splash in some soda water.

Pour into large wine or old-fashioned glasses, letting a little of the fruit fall into each glass.

I've learned that self pity is a waste of time

Chapter Sixteen

Sweet Rolls and Attic Trolls

After a long day on the farm, the evenings were for relaxing. A little television or my grandparents would read and share stories from the Reader's Digest, a publication that could be found in every room of the house. When Gram died, we discovered a bookcase filled entirely with decade after decade of these pocket-sized volumes. A good story or a funny anecdote never falls out of fashion.

Most children would do anything to avoid the inevitable call for bedtime. Not me, because I knew that just before bedtime was the best time. Second dessert.

It wasn't anything grand. No slices of pie or cake. Often it was stewed rhubarb with toast and butter. Or a dish of applesauce and a digestive cookie. If we were really lucky, some ice cream or a slice of a sweet loaf. It wasn't the treat or the sugar rush before hitting the sheets, it was the comforting ritual at the big kitchen table with Gram beside me

We'd stare out into the dark through the picture window watching for headlights and making guesses as to who they might be and where they were going. It was twenty minutes of quiet conversation and sharing thoughts and dreams in the comfort of our pyjamas.

At the top of the farmhouse were two bedrooms, plus the sewing area and the attic. To reach this space, you had to climb a tall wooden set of stairs. The stairs were glossy and slippery in stocking feet. We were always warned to be careful going up to bed because it was a long fall back down to the bottom of the staircase.

By the light of day, nothing in that house would be scary to a kid. It was warm and familiar, until the lights went out.

The smaller bedroom had double beds and a window. The bedspread quilts were sewn by Gram. The sheets were clean and crisp and smelled of the country air. There was often another sibling in there to keep you company.

The larger bedroom had a tall double bed and with a massive wooden headboard. The set once belonged to my great-grandfather Millard. It had a white chenille bedspread that looked like it had freshly popped popcorn sprinkled over it. More importantly it had a brass reading lamp over the headboard for immediate illumination should any monsters decide to crawl from underneath that giant bed or worse, out from the adjoining attic. God help us all, the attic.

There was truly nothing sinister lurking behind the tiny door that opened into the attic, or so Gram would tell me. But I saw a door just big enough for a demonic troll to casually walk through and climb up on to the end of my bed. It was worse knowing that if you sat up you could see the door. My eyes would play tricks on me in the dark and the door would look like it was open a crack. It was terrifying knowing my feet were close enough to the end of the bed that I could be pulled out from underneath the chenille bedspread and dragged into the attic before I could ever scramble to reach the lamp switch. No one would ever know I had been snatched away into the secret world within the attic until I didn't show up for breakfast.

Yes, the adjacent attic was definitely a frightening aspect to the room. Gram tried hard to remove the mystery. She would invite me in, trying to coax me with the treasures inside. The attic smelled like mothballs and stale air, exactly what a troll would prefer I thought. While I never once saw a demonic pair of red eyes peering out from behind a box of Christmas decorations, I didn't need to see them to believe that evil was lurking. Overactive imagination or not, if I knew I was sleeping in the big bed, I'd drag out that pre-bedtime snack for as long as possible.

Stewed Rhubarb

10 Cups Chopped Fresh Rhubarb
1 Cup Water
2 Cups Granulated Sugar

In a large pot, stir together rhubarb, water and sugar.

Simmer for 2 hours, stirring often, until rhubarb is soft.

You may want to add a little more sugar to your taste, depending on how sour the rhubarb is.

Allow mixture to cool. Pour into jars and freeze what you're not eating immediately. Stays good in the fridge for three days.

*Serve over vanilla ice cream or with a cookie on the side. It's also good troll repellent.

I've learned that violence on T.V. and in the movies is so graphic + extreme that its numbing our children to pain + suffering in the real world

Pumpkin Bread

3 Cups Brown Sugar
1 Cup Vegetable Oil
3 Cups Thick Pumpkin (Not Pumpkin Pie Filling)
$^2/_3$ Cup Water
4 Eggs Beaten
3-$^1/_3$ Cups Sifted Flour
1 Teaspoon Nutmeg
1-½ Teaspoons Cinnamon
1 Cup Raisins

Preheat oven to 350°.

Combine all of the dry ingredients (except raisins) in a bowl.

Combine sugar, oil, eggs and pumpkin in a large bowl until well blended.

Add the dry ingredients to the wet ingredients.

Fold in raisins.

Mix until well-blended but not over-mixed.

Divide batter evenly into 2 greased and floured loaf pans.

Bake for approximately one hour or until a cake tester comes out clean.

Great Grandma Millard's Maple Syrup Cake and Devil's Cake recipes.

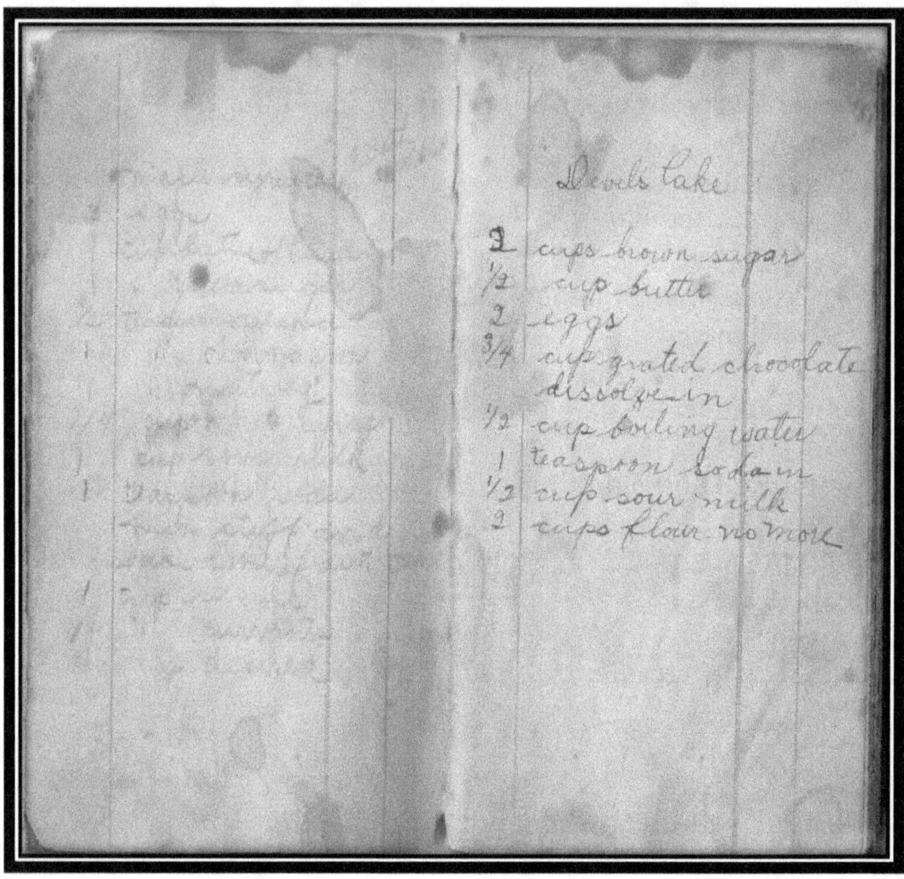

Zucchini Bread

3 Large Eggs
2 Cups Brown Sugar
1 Cup Vegetable Oil
2-½ Cups Grated Raw Zucchini
3 Teaspoons Vanilla
3 Cups Flour
1 Teaspoon Salt
1 Teaspoon Baking Soda
¼ Teaspoon Baking Powder
3 Teaspoons Cinnamon
1 Cup Coarsely Chopped Walnuts
½ Cup Raisins

Preheat oven to 350°.

In a large bowl, beat eggs. Add vegetable oil, sugar, vanilla and zucchini and mix well.

In a separate bowl, blend together flour, salt, baking soda, baking powder and cinnamon.

Stir the dry ingredients into the zucchini mixture until blended. Do not over-mix.

Stir in walnuts and raisins.

Pour into two greased loaf pans and bake for one hour or until a toothpick comes out clean.

Allow to cool on a wire rack.

Chapter Seventeen

If you're ever in a jam, here I am
If you're ever in a mess, S.O.S.
If you ever feel so happy you land in jail, I'm your bail
It's friendship, friendship
Just a perfect blendship
Friendship, Johnny Mercer

Carm and Marg Newell, Sid and Grace, 1955

I'm not sure I've ever met anyone who had longer and more valuable friendships than my Gram. She was the linchpin that kept the friendship wheels turning. For over 50 years, she was a member of the Good Companions Club. formed in 1948 by ten young married Ingersoll ladies. They composed a theme song, took minutes of their meetings, and created fun social and charitable activities to look forward to every month.

Over the years, the Good Companions grew to over 30

members, as new friends joined. Their friendships formed bonds that lasted decades and generations. When my Gram passed, she left me many skits and plays that they had performed together. If anything, she was a born entertainer and a bit of a comedienne.

The Good Companions didn't meet to just let off steam, they gave back to their community by having raffles, donating funds to furnish hospital rooms and provide treats for Meals on Wheels programs among other things.

There are names that I heard dozens of times through the years. Like that of Irene Noe, a dear friend of 60 years. She was their small town fashionista and a wonderful baker who had created many of the recipes in Gram's recipe box.

Friendships were important. I try sometimes to picture Gram on Instagram or Facebook, sharing memes and gossip dressed up as news. I think she'd quite like the immediacy of engagement but would tire of the excessive waste of precious time.

The people who don't believe in hell have never tried to get bubble gum out of a mohair sweater

Irene Noe's Pecan Pie

3 Eggs Beaten Slightly
1 Cup White Sugar
¾ Cup Corn Syrup
1 Teaspoon Vanilla
$^1/_3$ Cup Melted Butter
1 Cup Pecan Halves
1 Unbaked Pie Shell

Preheat oven to 350°.

Mix the eggs, sugar, corn syrup, vanilla and butter. Pour into an unbaked pie shell.

Top with pecans.

Bake for 45-60 minutes.

Allow to cool on a rack. Serve with a dollop of whipped cream.

This filling can also be used for tarts by replacing the pie shell with tart shells.

I've learned, no matter how thin you slice it there's always two sides

50th Wedding Anniversary Speech
Grace Roberts - November 1986

Neighbours, friends and relatives. I want to welcome you here tonight. I just can't believe we have made it to the 50 year milestone. In fact, the morning after we were married I had doubts if we would make through the first day. But we did and here we are.

Through these 50 years, we have been greatly blessed with wonderful neighbours and wonderful friends and last but not least family that has made our lives a real adventure.

They are loyal and supportive and we love them a whole lot. I've heard it said that the richest person in the word is not the one who has the first dollar he ever made, but the one who still has his first friend.

Some of you are friends from years back and some not so long, but each and every one of you have enriched our lives more than I can say. We do thank you.

Now, I want to say something about this guy I've shared my life with these 50 years. If I've ever accomplished anything, he is responsible. He has given me encouragement, understanding, patience and love. Yes folks, I've had the best.

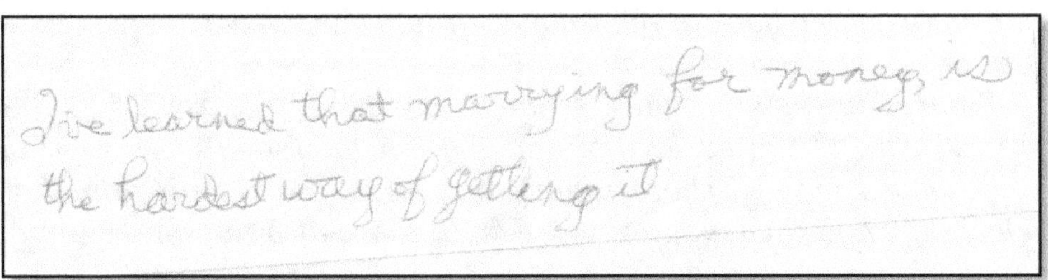

Another lifelong friendship was with Margaret (Marg) Newell, who was like a sister to Gram. She and her husband Carm were a part of my grandparents' lives for 55 years. This is the speech she wrote and shared at their diamond anniversary celebration.

60 Years
Marg Newell - November 3, 1996

Grace and Sid, what can we say? The big '60'! What a wonderful and memorable occasion. As our young people would say, this is "awesome."

Carm and I have had the good fortune to be counted among their friends for 50 of those years. Since 1946 to be exact.

After Carm arrived home from overseas, we moved from Woodstock to Ingersoll where we had purchased a home on Cross Street, unknowingly across the road from Grace and Sid.

I think we must have looked this house over on a sunny day. But when we moved in on the 1st of September in pouring rain, much to our dismay, I believe every room in that tiny cottage leaked. I was eight months pregnant and the house was damp and cold. The gas company had not come to turn the gas on so we had no way of cooking a meal. When what to our wondering ears, we hear a knock on the door.

A very handsome gentleman greeted us with a kettle of corn and a pot of steaming coffee.

Carm and I knew at that moment they were a special couple and our kind of people.

Close to Christmas, we met again on the bus downtown one evening and were invited back to their home for lunch when we discovered the four of us had a love of dancing.

From there our friendship mushroomed and strengthened. It started with a mutual love of dancing but we found we shared the same values and also shared a Christian faith, a solid foundation for a friendship. And the laughter: we seem to share also the same brand of humour and it comes so easily.

It's true, elderberries can have as much fun as younger berries.

We have had so much fun over the years but Grace and Sid are always there for their friends in the supportive times as well. I expressed these following thoughts on the occasion of their 45th anniversary. The same holds true on their 60th. Carm and I feel so comfortable with Grace and Sid. We can pour out our thoughts and words just as they are, chaff and grain together, knowing Grace and Sid will sift them, keep what is worth keeping and with a breath of kindness, blow the rest away.

Grace and Sid are man and wife but to the utmost they are also each other's best friend. This ingredient has to be at the top for a successful and rewarding marriage as is evidence on this their 60th anniversary.

Grace and Sid are truly blessed with the gift of making friends and it is one of God's best gifts. I would like to close with a little story.

Two small boys managed to miss the bus home from school. They were six miles away. The younger boy began to cry but the older who was only eight himself, took hold of his hand and said "Come on David, it's only 3 miles each." Off they marched together.

I thought after reading it, isn't it true that the road of life doesn't seem so far if you have good friends to accompany you along the way. Thank you, Grace and Sid for being that kind of friends. As Bob Hope would say, "Thanks, for the memories."

Thanks for the memories you have created among your friends and family, and for the memories you are still creating. And I highly suspect the sentiments Carm and I are expressing here tonight echo the sentiments of all your large circle of friends. God bless you both and we all love you.

Dancing was such a big part of my grandparents' social life, especially with the Newells. Whenever they could afford to get out for an evening on the town, they would head out to their favourite haunts. Ticket stubs to the Royal Muskoka, the Stork Club and the Highland fill Gram's old scrapbooks. So long as there was a big band playing, preferably Guy Lombardo and His Royal Canadians they'd find a way to be there. Back then, going out for an evening was an event. A new dress. A pressed suit. Dinner and dancing with the person who made your heart flutter, even after so many years. It was but one of the elements to their happy marriage. A friendship that lasted 74 years.

Marg and Carm Newell, Grace and Sid at the Highland in 1955.

Directions
Grace Roberts - 1980

Sometimes I like to reminisce of the days when I was a kid. One of my fondest memories was of my father and our 1920 Ford Touring car. He would climb in behind the wheel with all the importance of a three star general but he absolutely refused to make a left hand turn. He said it wasn't safe to take his hand off the wheel long enough to signal whoever might be following. However, in the 20s, there was hardly ever anybody following. To make matters worse my father would never ask for directions anywhere. He contended that the only way you learn is by figuring it out for yourself. The result was we were very often in the wrong place at the wrong time. After drunk drivers and Halloween pranksters who stole detour signs my father was the number one menace on the road.

Before I exchanged wedding vows with my husband-to-be, I jokingly said "Don't look upon marriage as a risk, but as one adventurous left turn." Somehow we never got around to exploring how he felt about asking directions until after we were married. We had circled a cloverleaf on the 401 in Toronto for hours. One day when I said "Dear, why don't you ask directions from someone?" he looked at me like I had just suggested he swim across Lake Erie and said, "I am not lost. "

"What do you mean you're not lost? To drive behind you is to See Canada First! Why are you too proud to admit you haven't the foggiest notion where you are?" I asked.

"Oh, you're just trying to start another argument" he said.

"I'm not trying to start another argument," I replied, "this is the same one."

"That's the difference between men and women" he said. "Women don't like to figure things out. As soon as they see a cow in a field they panic and right away start asking for directions."

That was to be the first of many trips where we wandered aimlessly about the countryside completely lost and too proud to ask.

True, we have stumbled upon things that ordinary people who know where they are going, never get a chance to see. There was Punky Doodle Corners, the Trillium Woods, Salford landfill and one

Sunday we even discovered the elusive Mrs. Tucker's Ice Cream Parlour and split a hot fudge sundae.

We've explored every dead-end road in the province of Ontario, some of them twice. We've blazed trails where only covered wagons have been and discovered the maternity ward of blood-sucking mosquitoes.

My husband is not unique. In talking with other wives, I have learned that there lies something in the male genes that breeds stubbornness and will not permit him to form the words "Could you please tell me how to get to such and such?" Men regard asking directions as a genetic weakness.

One thing I do know, my husband will go down in history with the other patron saints, not lost, but never really found. Like Christopher Columbus, Dr. Livingstone, Wrong Way Corrigan, etc. etc.

I often asked Gram what her secret was to a good marriage. It seemed to me as I was growing up that marriage was a temporary commitment, that perhaps we as a society no longer felt compelled to put the work in to make it last. She told me her secret.

"The secret to a good marriage is to treat it like a good garden. A good garden and a marriage must be nourished every day. Never go to bed at night angry with each other. Keep the weeds out of the garden and the marriage: they interfere with the most important things. Be patient. A marriage needs patience, and you can't expect a garden to blossom and produce overnight. Be considerate. Leave some space for the other person. Be forgiving, encouraging and loving."

Poppa Sid told me that Gram "has been a wonderful wife and a great caregiver. Our talks over breakfast and any other time of the day are just great. If I had it to do again, I would do the same. Really, I could go on for two or three hours. She has been my great inspiration and a wonderful homemaker for me."

Their lives weren't perfect. I'm sure there were times over the years when they struggled. However, I never heard either of them say an unkind word to or about each other. The level of trust and respect they had for each other was uncompromised. They were each others' best and truest friends. Of all the lessons I learned from my Gram, her lessons about marriage have been the ones with the most beneficial impact.

A Valentine from Sid to Grace, early 1960's.

Chapter Eighteen

I'm as busy as a spider spinning daydreams
I'm as giddy as a baby on a swing
I haven't seen a crocus or a rosebud or a robin on the wing
But I feel so gay in a melancholy way
That it might as well be spring
It Might As Well Be Spring, Rodgers and Hammerstein

In Ontario, most varieties of robins fly south in October. The harsh winds of winter are not welcoming to these fine feathered friends, but every year they return.

Early spring, I would wait for her call. Usually near the middle of March when the snow was finally melting and wisps of green were showing on the branches, the ring would come.

I would answer the phone and she'd say "Sheryl? Is that you? I saw my first robin today. Spring has arrived!" Every year, as consistent as a birthday. A calendar wasn't necessary if a robin was spotted. Crocuses and tulips were coming soon.

Gram spent a lot of time teaching me about different birds and the calls they made. There was never any shortage of colourful visitors in the trees on the farm, but robins were one of her favourites. Their return represented something new was coming. Growth and familiarity all at once. For a woman who lived through wars, suffrage, the Great Depression and all of the other tragedies that can befall a woman in 98 years, finding joy in a pretty bird arriving on your doorstep is a simple pleasure.

Gram's death, even at 98 hit me very hard. I knew it was coming and she left this world on her own terms. She was more than ready to meet Poppa Sid in heaven. She missed him so. Even with time to prepare I was still lost and I grieved for a very long time.

One particularly difficult morning in late October of the year she passed, I was walking to work from the bus stop around 7:30am. The city was still fairly quiet as rush hour hadn't quite begun. I was slowly and sadly walking down of all places "Easy Street" as I headed to the radio station where I worked as a copywriter.

Temperatures had dropped quickly overnight and frost was glittering on the fallen leaves and asphalt. I remember wishing that I had worn my gloves because the nip in the air was doing nothing for my sour mood.

As I walked, I looked to my left and my eyes landed on the most extraordinary sight. On the front lawn of this home on Easy Street was not the usual one or two robins getting ready to head south but about a hundred robins. A flock, all males with their red breasts puffed out, cocking their heads listening for their next meal.

I stopped in my tracks. Never before had I seen so many robins in one place at one time. Perhaps it was Mother Nature just doing her thing but maybe this was something more. Hot tears sprung to my eyes. Maybe this was a message.

Perhaps this was Gram's way of saying "Stop your moping, Sheryl. I'm where I want to be. I'm happy. You should be too." If anyone could harness nature to do her bidding it would have been her.

Now I know that we can create whatever narrative we want when we need it to make us feel better. This could be my circumstance too. The takeaway is that it worked.

I'm blessed with a reminder of her love and spirit for eight months of the year. Reconciliation between our brain and our heart is often right before our eyes. We have to be open to seeing it but more so, believing it.

Sheryl Rooth

"Gram" I asked, "What's the secret to a long life?"

"How would I know the secret to a long life? After all, I'm only 85! Okay...eat right. Have a sense of humour. Laugh at nothing. Smile at old folks and babies. GO TO CHURCH. We all need a little religion in our souls.
Keep busy and be optimistic. Amen."

My Gram, 2005

134

Substitutions

1 Tablespoon Cornstarch	2 Tablespoons of Flour
1 Cup Sifted All Purpose Flour	1 Cup + 2 Tablespoons Sifted Cake Flour
1 Teaspoon Baking Powder	1/4 Teaspoon Baking Soda + 1/2 Teaspoon Cream of Tartar
1 Cup Milk	1/2 Cup Evaporated Milk + 1/3 Cup Water
1 Cup Buttermilk	1 Cup Milk + 1 Tablespoon Vinegar or Lemon Juice
1 Cup Molasses	1 Cup Honey
Vegetable Oil	Unsweetened Applesauce

Equivalents

1 Tablespoons	1/8 Cup
4 Tablespoons	1/4 Cup
8 Tablespoons	1/2 Cup
16 Tablespoons	1 Cup
2 Pints	1 Quart
1 Quart	4 Cups
4 Ounces	1/2 Cup
8 Ounces	1 Cup
2 Cups	1 Pint
2 Cups Sugar	1 Pound
3 Teaspoons	1 Tablespoon

Thank You

Carol Roberts - Thanks Mom, for filling in the gaps and putting faces to names in the photographs.

Gerry LaHay - Thank you for your encouragement. I'm sorry you didn't see me to the finish line but I know you're here in spirit.

Kelly Lynne Elliot - Thanks Kelly, for your farm wife perspective and for being an amazing woman in politics, lighting the way for others to follow. Gram would have really liked you.

Sarah Gastle - Everyone should have a sweet soul like you to call a friend. You are all the Vitamin D a person will ever need.

Laurie Bursch - Editor extraordinaire! Thank you is never enough.

Jerry Colwell - I appreciate you and your preposition rules.

Shaw's Ice Cream

Wrigley Canada

Kraft Canada

Maple Leaf Foods

General Mills Canada

Kellogg's Canada

Tillsonburg Historical Society

The London Free Press

Newark District Community Cemetery

J. Clark, Ottawa Ontario

A certain man wanted to live to be a 100, and he was advised by his Doctor to give up drinking smoking + women. Will I live to be a 100 then? asked the patient "No," said the Dr. but it will seem like it